A Tribute to O'Hara
. . . and other stories

by

Christine Goldbeck

This book is a work of fiction. With the exception of John O'Hara, any references to historical events; to real people, living or dead; or to real locales are intended only to give the fiction a sense of reality and authenticity. Characters, and incidents either are the product of the author's imagination or are used fictitiously, and their resemblance, if any, to real-life counterparts is entirely coincidental.

A TRIBUTE TO O'HARA AND OTHER STORIES. Copyright 2000 Christine M. Goldbeck. All rights reserved. Printed in the United States of America. No part of this book may be used or reproduced in any manner whatsoever without written permission except in the case of brief quotations embodied in critical articles and reviews. For information address Christine M. Goldbeck, 39 E. Centre St., Shenandoah, Pa., 17976 or cgoldie@epix.net.

Cover and book layout designed by Christine Goldbeck and Jim Skinner
       Art by David Naydock

Published in the United States of America by McKeever Publications, Lutherville, MD.
Printing by Thomson-Shore, Inc, Dexter, MI.

ISBN: 0-9643905-2-3
Library of Congress Card Number: 00-191815

Praise for "Tribute"

I didn't want it to end. Skillfully perceptive. Professionally composed. Truly a masterpiece of eloquence. -- ***Dr. John Devers, author, The CoalCracker.***

*F*rom the light-hearted but pointed fantasy of the title piece to the hilarious but totally real neighborhood bar habitus in "Proud to be an American" to the very believable three Cait Beck stories in which a "sandwich generation" woman must deal with the sudden death of her middle-aged father, a grandmother's Alzheimer's disease and questions from a fiercely bright little daughter in whom she sees so much of her own self as a child, Christine Goldbeck put it all down right. --***Ethel Manning, Pottsville Republican and Evening Herald***

I just love those stories, especially "Black Dirt." I knew an old woman in Ireland who had a son in America who never visited her, or wrote to her. But she talked about him every day. My own uncle left home at 17 and never came back or wrote to his parents, who still talked about him until the day they died. Your stories have universal themes: you easily reach out to me from another generation and another country, and you would be understood by people everywhere because you write about things they understand.
  – *Patrick Campbell - columnist and author of "A Molly Maguire Story," "Tunnel Tigers" and other titles.*

Anyone who comes from a small town anywhere will enjoy it. The first half is a series of stories that illustrate the lives of the hard-working people who either live in or hail from the coal region. My favorite of these stories is "Black Dirt," In Book Two, Cait Beck, the stories continue, but are told from the perspective of a woman who grew up and still lives in the coal region. Cait reminisces about life with her father after his death; struggles with caring for an aging (and crotchety) grandmother; and strives to instill positive values in her young daughter. In "Dress Rehearsal," Cait's grandmother meticulously, and demandingly, instructs her on how she would like her death celebrated, as they both attend the wake of one of the town's well-loved Irish gentlewomen.

I am not from the coal region and I enjoyed this book immensely. It is emotional, and inspiring. It will make you cry, as well as chuckle. I can't wait for the next one! -- **Kerry Golden, Middletown, PA.**

We are bound
as the birch
to the coal banks
Our roots embedded
in the black rock
on which we build.

Christine Goldbeck

Dedication

With love, this book is for Rebecca. May she know that all things are possible if one trusts in what one loves and follows it through.

With love, this book is for Jay. May he forever know how his encouragement, enthusiasm and his listening skills inspired me to pursue my dream.

With gratitude, this book is for Eric McKeever, Gary Martin, Tommy Symons and fellow coal region writers who listened and encouraged. Thanks also to teachers who nurtured my love for the written word, especially Barbara Sninsky.

With coal region neighborliness, this book is for the countless people and regional places that I will forever hold dear.

Contents

FOREWORD

BOOK ONE – THE SOUTHERN FIELD

A Tribute to O'Hara 3
Proud to be American 17
Soul for Soul 29
Black Dirt 37
Midnight Revisited 67

BOOK TWO – CAIT BECK

Ripple 83
Autumnal Awakening 91
Dress Rehearsal 111

Afterword 139
About the Author. 143
About the Artist. 145
Recommended Reading . 147
Internet Links. 149

Foreword

In a unique and delightful tribute to the famed author John O'Hara, Christine Goldbeck imaginatively brings him back to life again briefly, to visit a high school literature class. This singular event takes place in his hometown of Pottsville, Pennsylvania, known as "Gibbsville" in his first great literary success, "Appointment in Samarra".

While at the school, he discusses how he was regarded in his hometown after he had become a famous author, and in the years following. O'Hara's personality and writing were both profoundly influenced by his growing up in this archetypal coal town in the hard coal regions of northeastern Pennsylvania. The anthracite regions were so vital in his memory he called the area his "protectorate".

In the other stories that follow, the reader is provided an intimate look into the family and social life of the plain workmen, the miners who dug the coal that fueled the Industrial Revolution in the United States. This work was both arduous and dangerous;

in the century when the coal industry rose to dominance, then declined, more 30,000 miners perished in this area. Many thousands more were injured, or died prematurely from black lung induced by breathing coal and rock dust.

The stories in this collection are deeply moving and powerful. They are a record and description of a way of life fast fading, but still not quite gone. From 1850 to 1900, waves of European immigrants swarmed into the coal fields to find work in the burgeoning mining industry. It was the age of steam, and coal was king. However diverse these immigrants in their languages, religions, culture and customs, they were unified in the drudgery and monotony of the toil in the coal mines. The safety signs were in 8 languages.

These coal towns are distinctive in the nation, in the landscape, architecture of the old towns, and in accents of speech, though this last is now disappearing in the younger generations. These stories will convey to the reader a sense of that uniqueness of place in a very memorable manner.

Eric McKeever

Book One

The Southern Field

> *Author's Note: John O'Hara (1905-1970) was born, raised and began his writing career in Pottsville, Schuylkill County, Pennsylvania. He wrote 16 novels, 402 stories and won many writing honors, including the National Book Award. The following story was written for submission to STORY, which sponsored a contest in which writers had to bring a celebrity back to life. I thought this was a great concept and immediately decided that O'Hara was my star. Interestingly, there is renewed interest in O'Hara's work. To echo words O'Hara once spoke to a group: "It's about time."*

A Tribute to O'Hara

Jenna Harris chewed another fingernail, knowing that she would be angry with herself for allowing Mr. Bumstead and his "Meet the Great Authors" course to push her to this point.

"Faulkner was a genius, was he not? As an example, he employed four different narrative voices in *The Sound and the Fury*," Bumstead said. "That is no small feat for a writer."

That's the whole point, Jenna mused. He WAS. So who cares NOW?

"Faulkner was a writer for his time," Bumstead droned.

Time. Jenna looked at her watch. If Bumstead was into talking writers and the times, why couldn't he have chosen to discuss Jane Hamilton, Joyce Carol Oates, Tom Clancy, Pat Conroy, Frank McCourt, Jane Smiley, Grisham . . . hell, somebody who could write and wasn't dead.

She stole a glance around the Pottsville High School Library. Most of her classmates looked as disgusted as she felt. Colleen Sullivan was the only exception. She seemed to know more about these dead men of the pen than even the scholarly, nose-picking Mr. Eugene Bumstead, Ph.D.

"Mr. Faulkner's contemporaries, great men such as Steinbeck and Hemingway and F. Scott Fitzgerald, for example, were consummate . . ."

Jenna looked up, disturbed at windbag Bumstead's sudden silence. Jenna saw that he was glaring at an old man who was approaching the teaching space Bumstead used as the stage for his subjective and lengthy monologues.

The tall stranger appeared angry, Jenna thought, noticing that her classmates seemed to perk up at the sudden twist that had breathed some life into Bumstead's class - a purgatory if ever there was one.

As he grew closer to Bumstead, the man tipped his hat to the teacher. "Consummate what, might I ask?"

"Sir, who might you be? Have you registered at the school office? All visitors must register, you know. We can't be too careful these days," said Bumstead.

"Since you quite apparently did not include me on your syllabus for this course, I have taken the liberty of interrupting your agenda by transposing myself upon it." Extending his right hand to the frumpy Bumstead, the man continued, "I, sir, am John Henry O'Hara."

Colleen Sullivan fainted in her chair, falling upon the shoulders of Brad Johnson, all-star stud of the Class of 1997. Everybody else looked indifferent, although the female students appeared somewhat jealous of Colleen, whom Brad was petting.

"John O'Hara?" Bumstead chuckled. "He's dead."

"No deader than Faulkner, Mr. Bumstead."

"Okay, Mr. ah . . . you can go back and tell Dr. Winston that you succeeded in unnerving me and causing a most unfortunate ailment for one of my students," Bumstead stuttered. "Class, woo-hoo, class, your attention please. As I was saying, Faulkner's esteemed contemporaries were consummate . . . "

"Storytellers. They were great fellows, no doubt. Nonetheless, your Mr. Faulkner and his friends have been recognized to the point of perversity among the literati while I, meanwhile, have apparently been forgotten - bequeathed to the attics of old ladies who still won't admit they once read me by candlelight behind a locked door. I tell you this is . . ."

"Mr. ah . . . Mr. . . . look, sir, if you don't leave, I shall have to notify the office that the police must be called. The joke has gone far enough."

"There is no joke. Mr. Bumhead, I assure you that I am John O'Hara. Look, if you will, in one of your encyclopedias. I am sure a photograph can verify my statement. Once we authenticate my identity, we can proceed with my agenda."

"This macabre incident is somewhat reminiscent of Ustinov's *Beethoven's Tenth*," Bumstead muttered.

"Ah, but I think I have better manners than the tempestuous Beethoven, although there are some, I am certain, who would not agree. What's more, we are talking classic authors not musicians and this is no Broadway drama. Besides, I think *Pal Joey* was much better all around than Ustinov's stuff. For starters, *Pal Joey* was original."

Colleen, stirring to Brad's gentle caresses, stared wide-eyed at the stranger. "Mr. Bumstead. He is O'Hara. I've no doubt he is O'Hara."

"Colleen, I think you had better visit the school nurse, I shall get some one to accompany . . ."

"Please, Mr. Bumstead. I believe him. To prove it, why don't we make him sign his name. Look, I have a copy of his signature here in this novel, one of his, of course."

"A bright girl, Bumstead," said O'Hara. Tearing a piece of yellowed paper from a tablet he pulled from his breast pocket and grabbing Colleen's Bic pen, O'Hara wrote his name. "Here, Colleen, please verify that I am me."

Bumstead rushed around the table to where the flushed Colleen was studying the signature. He grabbed her book and the piece of paper and peered intently through his bifocals. "Undoubtedly, these are written by the same hand, Bumstead said.

"Still, this is a most unusual, if not completely unbelievable, situation, Mister... well, Mr. O'Hara. Wouldn't you agree?"

"No. What is most unusual, Mr. Bumstead, is that you snubbed Pottsville's native son by not including him among those whose works your students are studying. What's more, good sir, you are boring these kids silly. Look at them. Faulkner? Good God, that's Mississippi, way down in Dixie. Steinbeck? California. Way the hell out of here, in more ways than the one presently under discussion. Meanwhile, here I am, under your nose and you do not so much as mention me on the reading list. Can you now see why I turned in the grave?"

"Holy Batman," Tom Stiles, class president, hollered, "I think this really is a guy back from the dead. Look at his clothes. Check out that hat. Look at the shoes!"

"My good fellow, I'll have you know this suit is a Wetzel."

"A what?"

'Suffice it to say that it is one of the finest suits money can buy."

Stirring from their Bumstead-induced comas, the students laughed. Jenna rubbed her eyes, thinking maybe there were hallucinogenic chemicals in the nail polish she ingested while ripping off her nails. On the other hand, she thought, if this were for real, then old Bumstead was going to get his comeuppance and the class was going to see a live dead author for a change.

Bumstead sighed. "I assure you, Mr. O'Hara, that I meant no disrespect. I have only eight weeks to do this class. Even you would admit that I am hard-pressed to divvy attention among great writers. There were so many of you . . ."

"But only one of us was born and raised in Pottsville. Only one of us is renowned for having created *The New Yorker* story. Only one of us has not been granted credit where credit is more than due, sir. And, while I can accept this of teachers in other places, I cannot accept this from a man whose grandfather was treated by my father, the good doctor. You, sir, have the power to acquaint me with a readership. You have the opportunity to entice Schuylkill countians to take another look at my work. Instead, you send them south, to Yoknapatawpha County. Tell me, sir, have you read me? Have you read *Appointment in Samarra* or *Ten North Frederick* or *The Lockwood Concern* or any of my multitude of short stories?"

"I've read of you, sir. Many articles have been printed in the Pottsville Republican and Evening Herald these last few years. They've been, for the most part, flattering."

"That is not the same as reading my work. Although, I must admit that Matthew Bruccoli, to whom credit is owed for keeping me alive, has done a fine job of exploring my mind. Nontheless, Mr. Bumstead, what have you done to make sure the Gibbsville Cycle of my work, as it has come to be called, is known among great, young minds such as these seated before us?"

Bumstead was silent. His face was reddening. He, cleared his throat, adjusted his glasses and wrung his hands. "I, ah . . ."

"Mr. Bumstead, if I may," Colleen interrupted.

Bumstead nodded for her to proceed.

"I have read and reread your works, Mr. O'Hara. I find your observations on the human condition of Lantenengo County to be most insightful," she said.

Jenna, like most of her classmates, rolled her eyes. Leave it to Colleen the studious. Where in hell was Gibbsville anyway?

O'Hara turned to Jenna. "Gibbsville, my dear, is my fictional name for Pottsville, your very own hometown. I trust that if you read my stories, you would enjoy recognizing the scenes and settings of Lantenengo County, which is none other than the Schuylkill County in which you live."

"Old stuff," Jenna retorted. "I don't see the sense of reading about such things if I live them every dull day. I don't need to be reminded that I live in the hinterlands. Why would I want to read that stuff when there is a world beyond this — a real world?"

"Jenna," Bumstead chided. "That was disrespectful."

O'Hara smiled. "Hardly. She poses a good question, which I shall gladly answer." Then, wagging his finger in the face of Bumstead, he bellowed. "You could be answering such questions yourself if you took the time to read and understand my work."

"Now, now, Mr. O'Hara, I'm sure you're on the shelf in fiction. Let us have a look, eh?"

O'Hara crossed the library, dodging reading tables and stopping to spin the big globe perched a top the wooden card file.

Mrs. Warren, the librarian, shot him a disapproving stare. The globe was not an entertainment prop for library patrons.

"And a good day to you as well, Mrs. Warren," O'Hara said. "Might you have any books by John O'Hara in this outstanding collection?"

"O'Hara? Which O'Hara might you mean? Fiction? Non-fiction?"

"That would be fiction, Mrs. Warren. O'Hara, John, 1905 to 1970, American writer of novels and short stories, born right here in Pottsville," O'Hara said. "Ever heard of him, Mrs. Warren?"

"Oh, sure. My mother said he was nothing but a liar. I remember her discussing him with her friends from the Hospital Auxiliary during afternoon tea. I distinctly recall the ladies agreeing. None of them had anything nice to say about him. They were glad he left Pottsville and went to the big city. They said . . ."

"Enough." O'Hara screamed. "Enough already. Where might I find his work in this library?"

"Look over in those stacks in between N and P. But, I warn you . . ."

O'Hara had already walked away.

"Why, Mr. Bumstead," Mrs. Warren said, "What is this half-dead, ignorant old man doing in your class? That man has the manners of a donkey."

"I assure you, my dear Mrs. Warren, that man is dead. Or back from the dead. He's O'Hara."

"Right," she said. "And, I am Currer Bell. I do believe you need a sabbatical, Mr. Bumstead. O'Hara. That's a good one."

The students, all but Colleen, laughed as Mr. Bumstead, hands in his trouser pockets and face toward the carpet, shuffled his way toward the stacks into which Mr. O'Hara had disappeared.

"Well, I'll be damned. No, I am damned," O'Hara said. "Most of these books haven't been read since 1975. That's 22 years ago. This is an outrage."

"I am quite certain, Mr. O'Hara, that if you visit the Pottsville Free Public Library, you will find volumes of your work are in frequent circulation," Mr. Bumstead said.

"You mean the library that banned my books for a time? I, sir, am quite certain that I remain under-appreciated. No posthumous glory for me, eh?" Shaking his head from side to side, he placed the hardbound copy of *Ten North Frederick* back on the shelf. "May I address the class?"

"You've already interrupted my work, Mr. O'Hara. Have your say. I rather think you would with or without my blessing."

Colleen's face glowed. The others, Jenna noticed, leaned toward O'Hara. Dead or not, he was undoubtedly more interesting than Bumstead.

"Your mentor, Mr. Bumstead, is quite correct. Faulkner was a genius. I said so myself in a 1949 interview with Harvey Breit for *The New York Times Book Review*. Therefore, he is important. Steinbeck is important. F. Scott is important. Hell, we're all important. As I told the crowd at Foyles Bookstore in London back in 1967, since I want you to feel that I am an important *something*, and as I am much too modest to insist that I am an important artist, I address you today as a social historian."

"Mr. O'Hara," I thought you were not keen on that tag."

"I was a novelist and a social historian only incidentally, Colleen. The United States in this century is what I knew, and it was my business to write about it to the best of my ability, with the sometimes special knowledge I still have. I wanted to record the way people talked and thought and felt, and to do it with complete honesty and variety."

"I believe you accomplished your goal, Mr. O'Hara," Colleen said.

Mrs. Warren, listening intently to O'Hara's speech, her mouth a gape, raised her hand. "But if you really are O'Hara, I've a bone to pick with you. You based your characters on real life people and embarrassed this whole town. You made money on poking fun of your own hometown."

"Not true, dear woman. My characters were not exact recreations of my friends. They were compilations of many people I knew here. Hell, while one half of town hated me because they thought I included them in my books, the other half despised me for not writing them into my works."

Bumstead was scribbling furiously in his little pocket journal. He was known to have moments of inspiration. Jenna watched tears pool up in Colleen's eyes. Mrs. Warren wore a look of disgust. There would be no changing her mind about John O'Hara.

O'Hara twirled his cane. "My dear, Mr. Bumstead, what are you writing?"

"Recording the incident of this afternoon, sir, so that I may write a story about it."

O'Hara laughed. "Are you insane? Who would believe that anyone came back from the dead?"

"But . . ."

"I have had my say. I have made sure I made the list of great authors discussed by your students. Now, if you will excuse me, as long as I am in town, I want to see a man about a whiskey, or two. No need to fear another hemorrhage, you know."

"Mr. O'Hara," Jenna said, "You never answered my question."

"Ah, Jenna, so I didn't. Pardon my oversight. The real world, my dear, is right here. The people and places and things around you are most interesting and worthwhile. Although the characters have changed since my day, and while I wouldn't be caught dead in the get-ups some of you wear today, their motives and this setting are not so different than the days when I roamed the streets of this town. Read and you shall see for yourself. As for me, I will die - - again - - and know that, despite the perpetuation of my name as the worst kind of scoundrel, I have left some mark on the world."

With a tip of his hat and a twirl of his cane, he turned and walked out of the library.

"Well, class, I don't quite know what to say. I don't quite know whether I believe what I just observed, or think I saw, for that matter."

Jenna raised her hand. "So, Mr. Bumstead, can we read that guy?"

"I suppose we must; however, I shall have to remove one of the authors from our list in order to do make room for O'Hara. The Good Lord knows this is going to be a challenge. I don't need Faulkner showing up here."

Proud to be American

All is quiet in here now. Bill, the proud owner of Blind Bill's Beef-N-Brew, is reading the obituaries in *The Fairlane Journal*. I nod to him and saunter to my customary place at the far end of the bar.

"Doctor Sam," he says, throwing aside the newspaper and rising to pour me a cold, frothy mug of Yuengling, the local beer. "Didn't expect ta see youze back so soon after the long night we had in here. Da wife is madder than all hell wit me. Says I gotta give up drinkin and socializin with the likes of you guys."

"Thanks, Bill. Get back to your paper and I'll sit here with my beer and my thoughts." Blind Bill is not sightless, and he does not serve beef. He sells beer and Kessler's whiskey. Only! Except, that is, for Fridays when Bill's wife cooks up bleenies and haluskie from noon until six. That's it! When it's gone, it's gone.

God help those poor souls who drop by looking for a sandwich.

"Don't serve nawthin else 'cause nawthin else matters here, youze know. Youze want that fancy stuff, youze can hitch a ride to The Penn Club out there on Snob Hill" is the explanation Bill recites when out-of-towners drop by for a drink and want something as exotic as a Beefeater Martini.

Blind Bill's has been here, and under the same name, for more than a hundred years. It was the miners' tavern when Langon Anthracite operated its mine and colliery on the western end of town. Call me sentimental or spooky, if you will, but I swear that sometimes I can hear the coughs of the men who spent their days in the belly of the earth and their nights in here, washing the coal dust from their throats and the fear from their hearts.

Bill says the bar has always been in the family. In fact, he refuses to die until his son, William Paul IV, "wises up and comes home from California to be proprietor of this fine establishment." Like young Billy, I am from here. I came back after my wife, a native of Boston, died. I shut down my thriving practice and came "home" to take care of coalcrackers and to take care of me. I've not regretted the decision, even though some times my friends in Boston accuse me of being crazy for wanting to live here. "These are my people," I tell them. "These are my roots. If people like me do not care, the place will continue to go downhill. The rebirth has to start some where, and it might as well start with me."

A draft beer costs 30 cents here in Blind Bill's. There's just no place like it left in Sylvantia, or even over in Miner's City or Ashville or up in Hilltown. The least expensive, next to Bill's, is 35 cents in Coalton, where the Irish drink in homage to Black Jack Kehoe.

Today, our older townsfolk say, this community, Sylvantia, a town once alive with more than 29,000 residents, is "going to pot." What they mean is that the place is going downhill. I am not certain they are right about this. I understand that they are worried about underage drinking, drugs, unruly youngsters, and the lack of respect for the town's ordinance on doggie business. I am concerned about their lack of understanding for our newest residents. Tiny was the one who brought the issue to the forefront in here, early this morning. The story is worth repeating because these fellas seem to forget that their antecedents were foreigners.

🕊 . . .

"Que pasa me ass!" Tiny stormed in shortly after 1 a.m. "Dis is unbelievable, don't youze think? For Chrissakes, I can't sleep for thinkin' about it."

Tiny stands taller than six feet and weighs nearly 300 pounds. He carelessly hung his flannel shirt over the back of his barstool and looked to see who was here to commiserate with him. It was a little hard to see through the smoky haze that had been building up for hours.

Bill's place is always open, but you will not find a soul in here between 4 and 6 a.m.

This is because Bill's wife, Freda, cleans the bar during these hours, and nobody wants to be near her. She "has a mouth," they say. Even Bill runs from his bride rather than listen to her complain about "men and their drinkin'."

"I couldn't sleep for trying, fellas," says Tiny. "I tossed, and I turned until I decided that a beer and a walk might make me tired enough to try the bed again. Yo, Bill, how about a cold one? Hey, that you, Stanley? For crying out loud, Bill, can't you buy a fan—or at least open a window?"

"Quit yer bellyachin', Tiny," Stanley hollers, his voice raspy from too many Camel cigarettes. "Vat's vorse dan the cigar smoke is da coal dust that ud be comin' in da vindow if it was open."

Stanley is a retired miner. People in these parts say he is as old as anthracite. Bill always serves his first several drinks in a soup bowl so Stanley won't spill whiskey all over himself. The old chap has the shakes until the first few drinks are in him. After that, Stanley is as steady as a soldier at attention. Visitors think it is difficult to decide whether Stanley is drunk or sober because he talks with the old country accent. He does not read or write English well. His immigrant parents, who came to Sylvantia to make a better life for themselves, raised him to speak his native tongue, Polish, first. English was a second language in the Towislawski household. It was used to communicate with others outside of the home, and only then.

Also here this morning were Clancy, who is out to prove the Irish can outdrink any other culture, and Smooth, the forty-something union pipefitter who is out of work and out to get those nonunion rebels from "way down in Dixie" who are building the coal waste cogeneration plant on the hill.

"If we'd a had nuclear power in the Civil War, none of dis would be happenin' now" is a statement Smooth often makes. In fact, like always, the subject was on his mind this morning. "Ah, Bill. Take my mind off my troubles with those doozies from the land of Dixie, will ya? Tell the story about the time we had visitors from 'the city' in here."

"Ya know, Smooth, I like the way Tiny tells that one. Let him whet his whistle, buy him a shot of Kessler's, and I bet he'll tell it again. He's gotta know it by heart now."

Tiny downed his pint and slid his glass down the bar to Bill. "Yeah, all right. Might as well. Cause pretty soon, I'll have to tell this yarn in that foreign tongue we gotta learn to speak in order to live around here these days."

"Vat's he talkink about, Bill?" Stanley looked confused.

"I'm not sure, old boy." But at least if he's telling a story, he won't be griping about whatever it is. Here, have another whiskey, Stan."

"O.K., boys," Tiny calls the bar to attention. "Hey, Clancy, wake up, will ya? Here we go. We all know how much Bill hates it when those rich ones come in looking for a menu. Well, one night, this couple finds their way to town after missing the Route 61 turn up in Mountain Vista. What a pretty pair they were. 'May we see a menu, sir?' the gentleman asked. 'Menu?' said Bill, his eyes as wide a Kennedy half-dollars. 'I ain't got no menu.' The gentleman gave old Bill here a funny look and asked how the beef was prepared and served."

... ✍

I was among the crowd here that night. Much to the astonishment of the dapper gentleman, and what appeared to be the red-cheeked embarrassment of his lady, the fellas at the bar burst into a chorus of chortles and chuckles. Tiny snorted beer out his nostrils, which sent the bar crew into an uproarious fit of gut-busting laughter.

Fortunately, the fellas realized that the city folk were offended and explained that they were laughing at the notion of Bill's cooking fine dinners—and not at the visitors.

🖎 . . .

"Well, I'll never forget the look in Bill's eyes, how about it? Remember when he said, 'Hey fellas, tell deez fancy folks how we be servin' up our beef here'? And Clancy shouted, 'Naw, Bill, youze tell them. This do be your place.'

"So Bill said, 'Well, then, O.K. It's like this, folks. Stanley over there, his beef is with his woman. Always nagging him to find a job so they can get offa welfare and be spectable people. But the guy spent years in the mines so he deserves welfare and Black Lung benefits, no matter what the missus says. And Tiny down there, his beef is with his boss, a good-fer-nawthin' fancy smancy biznis man who dresses kind of like youze do in your Sunday best Monday through Friday, though. Man ain't got the time of day for the kind of folks who help him make his money. And my beef, well youze ain't got the time to hear all my beefs so youze better head right back to wherever youze come from, youze hear me?'

"The man and his lady friend looked at old Bill, looked at us with our bellies up to the bar and our ass cheeks hanging off the stools. Then they looked at each other like we was all nuts or something ...Hey, Bill, another pint ought to get me through the story."

Sure, Tiny and his drinking buddies thought this was hilarious. However, I felt embarrassed when that nice couple stared at us as though we were aliens. We aren't. We're coalcrackers. Even Bill, although he's not among our most hospitable.

Without a word, the man helped his lady with her Italian lace wrap, and they headed for the door, leaving full glasses of beer and two one-dollar bills on the table.

"O.K., I'm ready to finish this tale now. So they go to leave, and Bill said to them, 'Hey, youze, wait, youze are forgettin' your money.' And the rich fella said, 'I assume that two dollars will cover the beverages.' Can ya imagine?

"'That and then some,' Bill told them. And that fella told Bill to keep the change.

"As soon as the door shut them out, Bill hollered, 'Hey, boys, the first two of youze who gits to the table can have them beers, but leave the bills. I'll be puttin' those into Father's collection at Sunday Mass.'

"'Those city people sure were dumb, hey fellas?" asks Tiny. "Two dollars for two glasses of beer? Incredible! Those folks must of been filthy rich—just rolling in the loot. Ah well, that's the way of it."

"Hey, Tiny, whatsamatter wit you? I hear you tell that story a lot better before," says Smooth. "Is the wife bitchin' again?"

"Shut up, Smooth. It's not my woman, for a change. Why I'm just sick to death of all these new people in town. Bums, the lot of them. All bums."

"Who youze talkink about?" Stanley guzzled another shot of Kessler's.

"Why, those Spanish people, Stanley. Jesus, Mary, and Joseph, youze can't believe what I went through today when Annabelle made me go with her to the bank, the post, and the food store. They are everywhere and always ahead of me in line. And they speak that foreign tongue!"

"Hey Tiny? Stop yer bellyaching," Bill hollered. "Old Stanley speaks different from us and youze get on fine with him. Here, let me fill that pint."

"Cripes, Bill! Stanley here is an American, for crying out loud. Yea, fill 'er up."

We drank on. Bill was watching CNN and talking about the impending apocalypse. Smooth fell asleep at the bar with his head sideways, mouth agape. Clancy belted down four more pints, stood up to relieve himself, and walked into the wall while singing the first few lines of "Danny Boy." Stanley stared into the haze and talked to himself about how the Irish and Welsh couldn't make pierogies with a Polish recipe.

Bill pulled the switch on the back bar at 3:45 a.m. Tiny knew it was quitting time. He stubbed out his Pall Mall, belted down a half-pint of Yuengling and belched.

"Going home before your missus comes down, Bill."

"Ganight, Tiny," Bill replied. "May god go with youze cause somebody's gotta be leadin' youze home to Coal Street."

"Vatch out for dem foreeners, Tiny."

"Night to youze as well. Yeah, those damn immagrants! What gives them the right to be here, of all places?"

❧ . . .

That was the way of it. There was no use arguing with Tiny when all that happened this morning, but I intend to bring up the issue with him this evening.

It's odd that I am still the only one here. Bill has finished reading the obituaries. He read the police blotter, too. I heard him mumbling about thugs and drugs.

I ask Bill where the rest of the faithful clientele are. Too early? Too late? Their wives got them doing chores?

"Hell no, Sam. Don't youze know tonight closes Forty Hours adoration? Even the Bishop is here. I'm surprised Father Shimisky didn't manage to fly in the Pope. Anyway, they'll be here shortly, but they'd all be at church right now."

Soul for Soul

"Officer Paul, when are you going to come to church?"

There he was. The good Father, trying to save another wayward soul. The priest shuffled toward Paul, who thought the old man should be saving his physical strength instead of souls. Maybe God gives Brownie points for bringing people such as himself back to church. Why else would a man as frail as Father be out on the streets of Sylvantia on such a damp morning?

No, Paul told himself as he awaited the Father's approach. God was too good for the Brownie point system. Now the Bishop, well he was another story. There was a Roman-collared coin collector for sure. Paul bit his tongue, thinking that he just committed himself halfway to hell for that thought. He made that remark aloud last year at a VFW wedding. Mrs. Norris threw a plate of steaming hot haluskie in his lap and told him he was the biggest sinner she knew. The least he could do is part with some of his Holy Communion money for the Bishop's annual appeal.

"Morning, Father. Where are you going so early?"

The priest struggled to regain his breath. "Och. Mrs. Smitowsky needs Communion, Tom Weakewicz wants his Last Rites. Again. Oh, and Mildred needs a bottle of wine for the Chicken Marsala. Damn it anyway! I haven't finished writing Saturday's sermon."

Father finally arrived under Paul's nose. Paul towered over the tiny man in the Father suit. His bullet-proof vest made his chest seem even bigger. He felt like Goliath.

"Father, you know if it wasn't for Millie, you would be eating Chef Boyardi."

Mildred Goodevich had been the rectory housekeeper ever since Paul could remember. God Bless Millie, he thought. She had survived the quirks of three priests in Paul's lifetime. It was common knowledge in Sylvantia that Saint Jorge's rectory was the cleanest place in the whole town. Why if cleanliness really was next to Godliness, then Millie had won her place in Heaven eons ago, townsfolk said.

"Yes. Well, Chef Boyardi doesn't need a $14 bottle of Marsala wine," Father shouted.

"Where's your Christian spirit, Father?" Paul taunted. The priest was so little that Paul had to bend his neck into his chin to see him. What he saw most prominently was the big bald spot on the crown of Father's head. The hairless flesh was drier than dead snake skin.

"I got a lot of Christian spirit, Paul Robersky. You, on the other hand, have not been to church since your mother's funeral. And . . ."

"Hey, Father, that's not nice." Sure, it was true, but he'd been busy working with the drug task force. Drug pushers do not observe Sunday Mass. In fact, Sunday morning is one of the busiest times for drug deals. With everybody else in church, they can peddle and push without the eyes of newsy neighbors upon them.

". . . And, come to mention it, you haven't been home the last five years that I came to bless the house. I had to bless the outside every year." Father was wagging a finger toward Paul.

"That's good, Father. Holy water takes the coal dust off the shingles."

Father seemed to grow about four feet after that remark.

"Now listen here, buddy. You're a smart ass. That's what you are! You've been a cop for too long. It's made you a horse's ass. What'dya say to that?"

Paul stifled a laugh and straightened his shoulders. "I didn't mean any disrespect, Father."

"Ah, sure ya didn't, Paul. Neither do any of the rest of them smart asses you call friends. Why you guys got an attitude. What do they call it, 'copping an attitude'?"

"Well, Father, I think if you saw the things I have while on the job, you would have an attitude too."

"I'm in the confessional every Friday. I don't get an attitude even when I hear things like . . ."

"Like Frank Yebowicz makin' it with Tom Frebowsky's wife, Father?"

"Where'dya hear about that already . . ."

'Hey, Father, this is a small town. I bet if we swapped stories, I'd have more dirt on the parishioners than you do."

"I'm not here to talk about everybody else's dirt. I'm talking about your dirt."

The pupils of Father's eyes were as big and as black as a chunk of anthracite. Paul worried that he'd pushed the kind old man too far. Lord, every Lithuanian in Sylvantia would kill him if he hurt their beloved priest. Father is more revered than Black Rock lager. In these parts, that is monumental. After all, this is a place where it would be difficult to say which is worshipped more, beer or church.

"Believe it or not, Father, I ain't got a lot of dirt."

"Sure, and Mildred can't cook. Even I have dirt." Father's stature shrunk. Paul felt relieved. He wondered if a person would go straight to hell for having a little fun with one of God's right-hand men. Granted, Father isn't the most reverent of priests in these parts, still, he is a priest.

"Sure you do, Father. You almost told on Frank and Agnes." Paul had tried to keep that remark from surfacing. But, once it reached his tongue, it had to come out. Like a kielbasa burp, there was no stopping it.

"Now listen, buster. I'm going to the liquor store; but, first, I'll ask it again. When are you coming to church?"

Holy Mary, Mother of God, Paul thought. Wife beatings, heroin addicts, nine-year-old burglars, . . . Church? Why it took faith just to believe that what he did on the beat every day could make a difference in the world. Church? Wasn't he saving souls? Wasn't trying to keep the Grabowski boy from lifting another pack of Kool 100s from Martin's Market saving a soul? Holy Jesus.

"Well?" Father stamped a foot on the concrete sidewalk. "Answer me. When are you coming to church?"

Looking toward the bell tower on Saint Jorge's, Paul saw that a fog shrouded his view of the symbolic cross, the beacon that had lighted his way when he was a boy on his way home from playing street hockey. The shining light he gazed upon every time he was on the return trip from the county jail, having delivered another parole violator, wife beater or drug addict back to the arms of the law. From way up on the Route 924 hill, the cross stood out, as though God himself was holding it in the air for all to see. Like a hiker clutches to rock to keep from falling, Paul eye's time and again had reached for that cross to keep from falling.

Paul refocused his attention to the tiny man standing beneath him.

"Well Officer, I don't have all day. You know, Saint Michael, the patron Saint of your business, might like to see you in a sacred place," the priest prattled as Paul fingered the silver Saint Michael medal worn beneath his shirt. Paul was never without the medal. Wearing it made him feel safer. There was someone good watching out for him.

Paul figured that God had to see himself and Father as two of a kind. This little man in the priest uniform was no different than himself. They were both in the same business, really.

"So, Paul, when are you coming to church?"

"Oh, how about when you pay your parking tickets, Father?"

Black Dirt

Francis McClare huffed as he slowed so as not to hit the pick-up truck in front of him. "Filth," he said aloud. "Already this ugly black dirt."

Honking his horn and scowling at the truck driver as he whizzed past him, Francis, or Frank as his friends back in Atlanta called him, stared at the man-made hills toward which he was driving. "I hate this place. It's been 42 years, and I still detest this dirty place."

He had not meant to return here at all; however, his younger brother Sean blindsided him with a guilt trip in a letter he received last week, just as he was scheduling his vacation to Greece. Sean had always been Mr. Reliable. If Francis wanted to knock off a day of school to go fishing, Sean had chided him about living up to the family standard.

Standard? Some standard. Squalor. Dirt. Francis sped up, not even bothering to take much of a look at the shops along Mountain City's main thoroughfare. It's not like anything around here could have changed. About the only change Frank observed, and he didn't have to leave his metropolitan playground do it, was Sean's demeanor. The tone of his letter was hateful.

You are a snob, Francis. You broke Ma's heart. She died whispering your name, you know. She prayed for you every day at Mass. She always set your plate at the dinner table on holidays. And you, selfish ass that you are, didn't even show up at her funeral. Didn't even send flowers.

Francis postponed the vacation, losing the lady who would have accompanied him. "Well, if those hicks are more important than me, then you just go, Frank. I've other things I can do," Barbara Ann told him. "You just run on back to that dirty place and eat those disgusting foods and drink Black Rock beer and sit around with a bunch of flannel backs."

When Francis pulled up in front of the house on Long Row in Gilbertsville, he turned off the Mercedes and leaned back in his seat. Two pick-up trucks and a beat-up 1970s-era Monte Carlo were parked out front. The dining room table at which he had eaten hundreds of meals was in the bed of a rusty old Ford truck. The china cabinet had been left on the porch.

Despite the shabby vehicles, the house looked like it had weathered the years well. The greenish asbestos shingling, a coal region architectural standard, was covered over by tan vinyl siding. The attached house, the Kosilowski family home, was dressed in the same color and style. Francis wondered where his mother found the money to refurbish the exterior. She certainly was not earning a lot of money from his father's Black Lung check or from Social Security. He did not think it likely that his mother, who had spent years working in the dress factory over in Valley City, received a pension.

Francis looked in his rearview mirror, pulled a comb from his visor and fixed his hair. Just as he was getting out of the car, a woman walked out on the porch and smiled his way. "Francis. Oh, Francis. It is you. I couldn't wait for you to get here. I thought you wouldn't be around until Wednesday. This is wonderful. Wonderful. "

He blinked. Was this little Patty? His baby sister? "Patricia? Well, I must say you've changed a great deal." Francis walked toward her outstretched arms. He felt queasy. Patty was merely a girl when he left, a beautiful red-haired, freckle-faced, laughing lass.

"Like you ain't changed a bit, asshole?" shouted Sean as he came out onto the porch.

"Nice to see you, too, Sean," Francis said, smiling so big that his mouth hurt. He'd be damned if this little SOB was going to do like he had done with his letter. No more guilt trips for Francis McClare IV.

Patty, smiling and crying, hugged him breathless. "You're a bad man, Francis, stayin' away all these years. Why you've nieces and nephews you have never seen. Oh, but, I've missed you. Sorely."

Standing there on the porch of his childhood home, Francis felt as though everything and, yet, nothing had changed in four decades. "It's good to see you, too. So, what's going on here? Is this moving day?"

Patty and Sean looked at one another. "You tell his sorry ass. I wish to God I'd never laid eyes on him. Some brother. Some son . . ."

"Enough already, Sean. He didn't come all this way to fight with you. Let's bury the hatchet, huh? Yours isn't any way to be treatin' a brother."

"Tell me what, may I ask?"

"Come inside, Francis. Freshen up. Have a beer. Ya had a long trip." Patty took her big brother by the arm and led him inside. Sean, his hands in the pockets of his jeans, his eyes glistening with unshed tears, followed.

🙞 . . .

Boxes were stacked in the living room, which still had the same white walls as when Francis was a boy. Francis shook his head. "She never fixed up in here, huh?"

"Oh we painted it several times over, Francis," Patty said.

"What's in the boxes?"

"Pictures over there," she answered. "You're welcome to go through and take what you want. We've took our fair share. Over in that corner are boxes of stuff Ma gathered during her lifetime."

Dime store decorations, Francis thought, and holy icons, statues of the Blessed Virgin and Baby Jesus, wooden crucifixes and years worth of palms. Those boxes were full of nothing that held any value.

"You know, thimbles, other bric-a-brac, really. I don't see you takin' interest in that stuff, but you may want some of the photographs, Francis ... for memories."

"Why would he want memories? Seems to me that's just what he doesn't want," Sean interjected.

"Sean McClare! Look here, we know you're angry, and I hope you boys can settle this mess you seem to be in. However, Ma would not like it that you were treating your brother like a dog, and that is what you're doing."

"It's all right, Patty. He'll get over it," Francis said, forcing his eyes to make contact with Sean. "I don't expect him to understand."

"Nothing you can think up will make me understand," his brother hollered. "You go off to strike your fortune and forget you even have family. We see your picture on television and in the newspaper, but never do we hear a word from you. Now that you've decided to show yourself, you're too late, Francis."

"What do you mean by too late?"

"Just what I said. Our mother is dead and buried, and everything that means something to everyone but you will soon be gone."

"I don't understand, Sean. It's not like anything here is worth something. By God, in Atlanta, a place like this is close to condemnation by the Health Department."

Sean turned his back and stared at the old pieces of furniture stacked against a wall. He cried more openly that most men will allow themselves in the company of others. The silence, the sniveling, was more than Francis could bear.

"Damn it, Sean. What's wrong?"

"Mind your mouth in Ma's house," Patty warned. "Sean is upset because of the problems with her estate."

"Yes, and there is no money to buy the solution, big brother. The place is up for taxes. We owe the funeral home three thousand smackers. They've turned off the electricity more than once and there isn't a decent chunk of coal to put in the furnace, save for what I scavenge."

"The place is up for taxes. You mean for sheriff's sale?"

"I do, brother. Ma died like she lived – with nothing. Patricia and me tried to help where we could, but it wasn't always enough."

"Francis, what he's trying to say is that I lost my job when the factory closed.

I'm just doing odd jobs for people to keep the kids in food. Maybe now that Ma has passed on, I'll go through job training and learn how to be a nurse's aide or some such thing." Patricia forced a smile. "Life goes on. Come, I've a pot of halupkie waiting."

Francis had not eaten stuffed cabbage (for this is what halupkie was called in the south) since he had left home. This had been one of his favorite dishes, growing up. He was surprised to feel his stomach rumble when Patty announced what she was preparing. "You go ahead and set the table, Patty. Sean and I will be along momentarily."

"Set the table. That's a good one, Francis," Sean sneered. Can't you see the damn thing's outside ready to be taken away?"

Francis waited until their sister was out of ear shot. "So, this is the reason for the nasty letter you sent me, Sean? You're all down on your luck? Well what of you? What do you do besides hold a grudge against me?"

"Down on our luck? No. We ain't that. If we were that, we'd be long dead, Francis. We're just in a rough spot right now is all." Sean sat on the floor and reached inside one of the boxes. He pulled out a handful of black and white photographs. "I'm sober as a judge now, Francis, and I'm back running shovel at the Richland mine."

Francis fiddled with the change in his pockets. "Did you have a drinking problem, Sean?"

"Have. Have a problem. One's too many and a hundred ain't enough. I'm working it through. Go to AA classes in Sylvantia Heights. Ain't had a drop of so much as cough syrup in 389 days. Mr. Richland was good enough to give me another shot at the job so long as I stay sober." Sean sifted through the photographs. "The sands of time . . . Oh, if only . . . Here, Francis, look at this one. You and me on the slag heap down back, across the creek."

Francis stared at his image, at the boy who climbed the coal waste banks more than 50 years ago and, at the time, loved every minute of doing so with his little brother. They were poorer than the dirt in which they played. Thank God I got out, Francis told himself, and then to his brother said: "Long time ago, Sean." Memories assaulted his thoughts – 1947 reclaiming coal cast aside by breaker boys, one of whom had been his grandfather McClare. Coal to burn at home. Coal to sell for 10 cents per 100 pound. Da choking . . . coughing . . . gasping for air. Ma crying. "Well, any way things are better now."

"Indeed they are. But Ma never could get on her feet. She tried. She was no quitter. She wasn't dumb. None of us are as stupid as you must think we are, Francis."

"Sean, I don't think you're stupid. Not a one of you. Foolish. Yes."

"Foolish?"

Francis felt something inside himself stir as his younger brother looked up at him. He sighed and sat down on the floor beside Sean. "Yes. Foolish. You know, Sean, I'm not the only one who left this place for better things. Practically three quarters of my friends did too."

"Yea, Francis, but they came back. Some just to visit on holidays, but they still came back."

"I've been busy, Sean. Very busy."

"That's a poor excuse for not even writing a letter. Besides, we all know different. You're embarrassed of us, Francis. So just admit it."

"All right, fellas. It's dinner," Patty announced. "Would you like to eat in here? Kitchen furniture is on the truck, so it's the floor for us no matter what room we eat in."

"Here is fine, Patty. Want help bringing it in?"

"No, Sean, I have it." She smiled. "By the looks of things you have mended the fence?"

Neither brother answered.

"Well then, at least maybe you're talking about it," Patty said and went back to the kitchen to get plates and fixings.

🐚 . . .

After dinner, during which she made small talk about her children, and the brothers said very little, Patricia cleaned the kitchen and went home. On her way out the door, she hugged Francis. "I'm just down the road at 301, the old Lewis place, if you need anything. The fellas will be here tomorrow afternoon, before I get here, to load up more stuff. There's no need to worry about the furniture on the truck. It's still the same, Francis. We still leave our doors unlocked in these parts."

Sean offered a curt "good night" to his brother on his way up the stairs. He stretched and rubbed his stomach. "Full belly," he said, cracking a tiny smile. It was the first happy expression Francis had seen on his brother in the two hours since he had arrived.

"Help you with something, Sean?"
"Nope. Going to bed."
"Oh. You live here?"

"Since Ma fell in 1990, yes. Sold my house in Coalton and used the money to fix up this place a bit. We put on the siding to match the house next door. She needed help tending the place. I wanted to put in an oil burner, but Ma wouldn't hear of anything except coal and an occasional wood fire."

"You never married, Sean?"

Francis saw his brother wince, as though stabbed. " Almost, once. She . . . well she left for a visit to Philadelphia and never came back to stay. Got herself a good job as a lawyer's secretary and later married the boss."

"I'm sorry, Sean. But, you see what I mean about me not being the only one?"

"Yea, deserters one and all. She died a couple years ago. I read about in the paper. Killed in a car accident on holiday in Germany."

"Well, good night, Sean." Francis tapped his foot. There didn't seem to be anything more he could say. "Oh, where should I sleep by the way?"

"You're staying here? Suit yourself. I have our old room. Ma's is the only one where there's still a bed. We haven't touched her room yet. Makes Patty cry. Gives me the willies."

"Is it okay for me to stay? I mean I suppose the house is yours now. So, may I stay here?"

"The house is the county's come Friday. Like I said, Francis, suit yourself. Stay where you want." Sean climbed the stairs.

"Good night to you, too, Sean," Francis whispered. "God, you think I'd killed someone by the way he acts."

Francis wandered in to the kitchen in search of a beer. He was certain that the refrigerator was the same one that had been there in '57, when he left. He grabbed a bottle of Black Rock beer and stepped out onto the back porch. Beyond the line of white birch trees, Valley Creek shimmered in the light of a full moon. Growing up, he and Sean used to swim in the creek, even though they had been forbidden to do so. "It's nasty old mine water," his mother would shout.

The slag heaps across the creek, the very ones in the photo Sean had handed him earlier, were smaller. Francis surmised the piles were being used for fuel at the new cogeneration plants, one of which was on the mountain beyond the slag. He had read about new coal technology in an issue of *Scientific Journal*.

Drinking the last of his beer, Francis wondered whether he should go out for a bit.

Take a ride over to Valley City? To Sylvantia? Thinking that he probably wouldn't know a soul anymore, Francis decided to call it a day. He felt drained and unsure whether to blame a long day of driving or the uneasy feelings he had about being here, of all places. Back here, a place he promised to forget because knowing it could only mean struggle.

❧ . . .

Upstairs now, he turned back the old quilt on his mother's bed and pulled down the worn window shade. The mattress sagged under his weight. The pillows smelled of lavender. Francis tossed. He turned. He opened his eyes. He closed them. Still, he saw his brother's accusing and hurtful eyes. *you're embarrassed of us . . . just admit it . . . you're embarrassed . . . just a rough spot . . . admit it . . .*

Francis settled on leaving in the morning. There was nothing to say. There was nothing he could do. He never should have come here. He should have ignored Sean's letter just as he had ignored those letters he had received back after he first left home to become a sailor for Uncle Sam.

Yes, dammit! He was embarrassed of this place and of his all-too-rough-and-tumble roots. Only a handful of people really knew the truth that he was born an anthracite coal miner's son in the black squalor of Fairlane County, Pennsylvania.

When people in social circles questioned his background, he would craftily defy talking about it. His childhood would never compare with the silver spoon club into which he had been accepted after rising to CEO at W. MacGregor and Company.

He had spent years in private speech instruction, learning to lose the coal region twang he had spoken. He learned to invest, to appreciate the finest single-malt scotches and to forget that he once lived in rags and picked coal to help keep his family in potatoes and oats. Until Sean's letter saying that Ma was dead.

So, here he was in her bed. Doing what? Francis felt like he was suffocating. He felt like his Da must have felt when he tried to breath clean air into his miner's lungs. Suffocating. That's what it was. This place sucked the wind right out of a person. If it was black underground, it was just as black above, what with dust swirling in the air like sand in the desert.

Why bother dusting, Ma? He used to ask her. *It's only going to stir up and settle somewheres else for crying out loud.* And she would tell him, *Francis, lad, cleanliness is next to Godliness. Surely the Sisters learn you that in school.*

Francis got out of bed and opened the window enough to feel the nip of the September evening air. In search of another quilt, he opened the blanket chest at the foot of his mother's bed. Instead, he found an image of himself, 40 years ago in his Navy dress blues. It was a newspaper photograph with word of his promotion to captain. Under this, he found more clippings. "Gville son meets Admiral", Miner's Boy Hits Paydirt", "Captain McClare at the Helm of Southern Electronics Firm."

Beneath the clippings, Francis found a clasp envelope addressed to Captain Francis McClare IV and bearing his mother's return address. There was even postage on the envelope, although the stamp had never been cancelled, and so, it had never been mailed. He took the clippings and the envelope to the bed. He felt even colder than moments before. So much colder that he shivered.

February 14, 1959
Dear Francis:
You sure do look handsome in your uniform. I am so proud of you, son.

Things are as fine as can be here at home. I still make dungarees at the factory. It's a good job and I've lots of friends over there to pass the day while we sew. Your Da gets around a little. He goes with Sean to the mine on days when his breathing is good. Some days, he just goes out back and sits in the sun from morning until night.
Patricia and Theo had a baby girl last month. They named her Fiona, after my mother. I thought that was nice of them, but I worry about the child because a name like that here might not be good. Seems they're naming babies all kinds of funny names, these days, the likes of what we'd never think of. Course we were taught to give our babies Christian names.
Sean works hard and plays hard, your Da says. I think that means your brother spends too many evenings at Stu's over in Coalton. I think Sean will be fine as soon as he finds a girl to fix his heart. He has not dated since Kelly Ann, who married a rich lawyer in Philadelphia. It's a long story. I'll tell you when you come home to visit. Poor Sean. He's such a good boy. Too good for the likes of some harlot like Kelly Ann. Soon as he turns his back, she runs off and marries a city boy.

Oh well, I sure am proud of you, son. I hope everything is well and that you soon come home for a visit. God bless.
Love,
Ma

She had included a photograph of his father, sitting in the backyard with his face skyward, soaking up light he had missed during his years underground in the damp, black hell of a deep mine. There were other snapshots as well: his sister with her new family, and one of Sean, in the living room with his harmonica to his mouth and his eyes dancing. Does he still play? Francis wondered.

Why had Ma never sent the letter? Francis turned the envelope upside down to spill the remainder of its contents. A recipe for bleenie, a chunk of coal, a twig of white birch, attached to which was a scribbled note, dated February 14, 1961.

Dear Francis,
I thought these things would remind you of how grand it is at home.
Love, Ma

Francis tried to feel mad so that he would not shed the tears he felt forming in his eyes. "This is crazy," he said. "Why didn't she mail these damn letters? Doesn't make any sense." *You came too late . . . embarrassed . . .* Francis picked up another envelope, this one more recently addressed to him as chief executive officer. He ripped it open. The handwriting was that of an old woman. It bore little resemblance to the strong strokes and curlicues in her previous letters. She may not have been educated past the sixth grade, but she could read and write as well as anybody who had been able to stay in school. It was one thing Francis now wished he could thank her for: her love of learning, her appreciation for the written word. *Ya gotta study, son. It's the only way to become something. It's the only way you're going to know the things you need to know to . . . well . . . to grow up a man.*

What had she really meant to say? Francis wondered of that day when he argued about doing his mathematics when what he really wanted to do was go fishing with the neighborhood boys.

February 14, 1998
Dear Francis,
Some times you have to face facts. So, I have long since given up on you coming home some time, even for a little visit. I used to dream about it a lot. I would have taken you over to

Finley's just to have every one see you in uniform.
Steve Shaffer comes home three or four times a year to help his Ma with house projects.
Willy Reed has come home to stay for good because his Ma went blind.
Willy says he is real happy to be back. He doesn't only take care of his Ma. He goes fishing and hunting and hangs out at the AmVets and the Legion evenings to have a couple of beers.
I'm getting old now. I guess I am trying to say that I am feeling old. My bones creak like the stairs in our house. Anyway, I want to let you know that Sean takes good care of me and Patricia does all my grocery shopping, cooking and cleaning. I go to seniors center to play cards and I get out to Mass and to your Da's grave almost every day still. I always say a prayer for you at church.
It's okay if you don't want to come home even though everyone thinks you should at least visit. I tell everyone that you often call and you're just very busy with business. You must be, right?
You take good care of yourself, son. I hope God is good to you.

Love,
Ma

Francis threw down the letter, written only last year, got out of bed and put on his slacks and shirt. He had to get out of here. Had to. Now. Surely he would suffocate if he did not.

🕮 . . .

He drove west on State Route 54, passing the old Saint Richard breaker and the patch towns, where he had played as a boy. The business man in him had to agree that the mine owners had a great concept in patch towns, or the villages the mine companies built near their collieries. Workers and their families lived in these company homes and shopped at the company store in the village. So what they earned in the mines, they returned to the men who employed them. Yet, the Irish Catholic in Francis knew what a hard life the miners and their families lived because he had lived it, too.

Just before Sylvantia, he pulled over to look at the new coal plant; a cogenerating station. Old and new technology were so close together. The old plant was within a short jog of this place. And in between were the old coal company houses, now privately owned. Some of these had been remodeled.

Others looked about the same as when he was a kid, save for a new front porch or storm windows.

In Sylvantia, Francis parked on East Centre Street, outside Blind Bill's Café and its flashing neon Black Rock beer sign. "What the hell," he mumbled, and went inside. Maybe he would run into some of the old gang.

"Lost your way, sir?" Bill, the owner, sat behind the bar, not bothering to get up when Francis walked in. Bill was not blind, though one of the Bills before him had been. The barroom had been in the family for generations. Somehow, it was one of the old miner bars that survived the changes that had taken place in the southern field.

"No. Well, yes, maybe so. Can a fella get a beer here?" Francis heard himself slip into the local vernacular. He shook his head, frustrated with himself.

"Sure can." Bill hopped off his stool, poured a draft for his customer and sat it on the bar. "Thirty cents."

"Thirty cents? Cripes."

"What? You think 30 cents is too much to ask for a draft of the best beer in these parts? Hell, go across town. They'll charge ya a buck for the same thing."

"No, that's not it. I'm rather shocked how low the price is, that's what."

"Folks here ain't so rich, Mister. Least not where money is concerned."

"I know."

"You know, huh? How you know? You don't dress like you're from these parts. You don't much talk like a coalcracker either. You almost sound like a rebel. You from Dixie? Shoulda let those states go when we had the chance. Ask me, they're useless. Government just keeps handing dem cotton and peanut farmers money. It's money should be spent here, helping to breathe life back into this place. A lot of friggin' thanks we get for fueling a revolution, huh?"

"I just know is all. Your place doesn't get a lot of people in, I reckon?"

"Wrong," Bill said and laughed. "They'll be back. There was a fire over on Oak Street coupla hours ago. The boys'll be back soon with a big thirst and plenty of stories about their heroics."

Francis smiled and sipped his beer. No doubt he had forgotten how good Black Rock beer tasted from the tap. It was available in Atlanta these days. Black Rock beer, the premium version and its other products, was the rage up and down the eastern seaboard. Francis, however, did not drink much beer anymore. He had taught himself to become a dry Manhattan man. Not today though.

Coming home had awakened a thirst. He gulped the rest of the beer in his glass.

"Ya drink like a coalcracker though," Bill said. "How 'bout another?"

Nodding, Francis placed a $10 bill on the bar, thinking that he could get more than drunk on that amount of money in here. "Hey, can I ask you something?"

"Shoot."

"A lot of people still grow up and leave here, do they?"

Bill's face went white. He refilled Francis' glass, took 30 cents off the bar and turned toward the cash register. As quickly as he had lost composure, he regained it. "Some. But not like they used to. Things are getting better around here. More industry. The cogeneration plants, a big warehouse for Lowe's, computer stuff. Things are looking up."

Francis had noticed the change in the bartender. "You okay? You don't look very pleased about the place getting better. Did I say something wrong?"

"No. You just hit close to home is all. My son left and never came home. Not yet anyways. I'm still working on him. Big businessman, he is. Doesn't have time to come home and visit his mother and father. This place made enough money to send him to Penn State University. He don't think of it as anything good though. Told me the whole county is a shithole."

Francis choked on his beer. He turned his attention to the television mounted on the wall behind the bar. He feigned interest in the news while he attempted to get rid of the feeling that his lungs were collapsing in on themselves.

"Say something wrong, did I?" Bill put his hands, palm down, on the bar and stared at Francis. "You a coalcracker, son?"

"I . . . I'll have another beer, thank you."

Bill saluted Francis. "Tell you what: this one is on the house. Welcome home."

The thought of drinking that beer soured his stomach. When Bill turned around to get a fresh glass from the cooler, Francis grabbed his change and left.

☙ . . .

Sean was gone when Francis woke up to the sound of birdsong, put on his slacks and went downstairs to the kitchen. He would have coffee and get on the road before anybody showed up. He had slept fitfully, waking in sweat from dreams no self-respecting, wealthy businessman should have. The worst had been the dream about the picnic at Coal Grove in 1949, when he was 10, Sean, nine, and Patty, five.

It was Da's mine company picnic. The mine owner was there, saying thanks to the employees for a successful year despite the odds. After all, anthracite mining had passed its hey day and Richland Anthracite was still going strong, stronger than the nay-saying company accountants had predicted.

"Da?"

"Francis, hush up and listen."

"But, Da, I want to tell you something important."

"What is it, son?"

"Da, I'm going to grow up and make more money than Mr. Richland ever dreamed."

Francis McClare III laughed and ruffled his son's curly, black hair. "You gonna have your own coal mine, son?"

"Whatever it takes, Da. Cause I'm going to buy Ma a wringer washer and I'm going to buy you new lungs."

Francis Sr. held back tears. "That's mighty thoughtful of you, Francis. I hope you grow up to be as rich as him up there. Even richer if that's what you want."

"It's what I want, Da."

In his sleep and just now, Francis lived the dream as though his father were standing there now. It was as fresh as Cowalick's kielbasa loaf on a Friday morning. "Damn it. Damn it." Francis threw a coffee mug, which hit the metal cabinet and smashed to slivers. "You made it, big boy. You made it all right. And you left them. You left them because you forgot who you are."

By noon, Francis had been through each room in the house, including the cellar, where he found his coal wagon. He had also been to the garret, where he found drawings he, Sean and Patty had made during their school years.

By 12:10 p.m., when he opened a bottle of beer and sat on the back porch in the sunshine, he felt sick. He knew he was wrong, knew he had been wrong for most of his life . . . *too late* . . .

Sean came home at 3:15, when Francis was on the living room floor, surrounded by photographs and the letters he had found the night before.

"You look like hell. Sick or something, Francis?"

"Sean, last night I found letters Ma had written to me but never mailed. Do you know of these?"

"Nope. Only thing I know is that she and Da never gave up hope that you would be back. Like I told you in my letter to you."

"Do you hate me, Sean?" Francis watched his brother walk past and in to the kitchen. He listened as Sean slammed drawers and cupboards.

If Sean did hate him, it was understandable. Francis didn't have a very high opinion of himself at the moment and was uncertain that he ever would again. Who had been the fool? These people were not fools. They were his blood. "Sean," he hollered, "you still play the harmonica?"

Francis gave up hope for an answer and went about sorting snapshots. He wanted to make an album for himself. He had not heard Sean come in to the room.

"On occasion, I do. Why?" Sean held his harmonica in his right hand.

Francis smiled. "Just wondered is all."

"This here's a standard C note I carry around. Upstairs, I got a whole set. Ma loved to have me play. I used to play in the bars all the time, too."

"I would really like to hear you. I remember you playing for us, and I recall it made Ma and Da very happy."

"Maybe later. I have to put more furniture out to the porch. Did anyone call? Bob Lingle was supposed to come and take the table and the cabinet that's outside."

"Nobody called. Haven't even seen Patty all day."

"She'll be around soon. Probably with the kids in tow. We usually all eat supper together. Those kids look just like our grandma and grandpa, Francis. It's amazing how looks go."

"Sean, where's the furniture going?"

"Some to Alvin Brink, the antiques dealer in Fairlane Junction. Some's being sold privately. We're using the money to pay off her bills."

"Are there a lot of bills?"

"Hospital. Electric. Funeral. Odds and ends."

"How much do you need to pay it all off?"

Sean's eyes fired bullets at his brother. "We don't want charity, brother, if that's why you came. You can't buy forgiveness. Money won't rid you of guilt."

"Knock it off. Okay, Sean? You're right. Okay? That what you want to hear? Fine. It's said. And, I'm sorry, okay? I was wrong. But so are you, because it is not too late. I can help. And, it's not charity. I'm offering because I'm selfish."

"Oh you're selfish, all right. I don't even know you. If you didn't look so much like me, I'd think you were a stranger. What are you offering?"

"I'll pay the back taxes at the courthouse tomorrow. You unload the furniture and put it where you want it. In fact, I'll help you." Francis put down the photographs, except for one that he handed to Sean.

"Hey? Remember that day, Francis? We come back with a wagon full of coal? Look at us, all black and happy after playing in the dirt."

Francis stood up. He extended his right hand to his brother. "All I want is occasional board in one of your rooms here, Sean. For when I come home to visit."

Sean smiled and extended his hand to Francis. "Deal."

"Deal. Now how about you play me a couple of tunes?"

"All right. Let me go get the fancy ones." Whistling, Sean bounded upstairs.

Francis worked at re-stacking photographs in a box. He noticed that his hand had been sullied in the shake with Sean.

"Black dirt." He grinned.

———— ✍

Midnight Revisited

Summer evenings in Fairlane County towns are community social hours. A day's work is done. As it has been for decades, folks come out to catch up on what has gone on in the lives of their neighbors.

After watching the local news, most men folk head off to the fire houses to commune with their fellow volunteers and friends. Children, their bellies full from dinner, spill in to the streets to ride their bicycles and play baseball, kick-the-can and hopscotch. After doing the dishes and packing tomorrow's lunches, wives settle in with a book or handwork. Many young mothers take their toddlers to the town parks.

Like fish on Friday and Mass on Sunday, this ritual endures the change that progress and technology bring. You can't very well feel the Thomas' baby girl on the Internet, after all. Certainly, it is cooler to sit on the porch than to plop in front of the computer.

Like their contemporaries throughout the county, Sylvantia's older women gather on their front porches to talk with neighbors and passersby. Sylvantia is one of the bigger towns in the region. So, there's lots to talk about.

Rocking in her ladderback at the front of 109 E. Centre St., Mary O'Connor sips her iced tea. Beside her, at 111 E. Centre, Margaret Rider gently sways in her own rocker. "Look, Mary, there's Mr. and Mrs. Ross leaving their office. It's pretty late for coal town lawyers to be working, ain't it?"

"Dunno, Margaret, maybe they're going to another Molly Maguire trial re-enactment. The last one brought in busloads of people. I still can't figure why anyone'ud want to come here."

"History. That's why. The Mollies made history. My dad always said it's because of them that miners got a little breathing space."

"Let's not fight, Mary, huh? You know how I feel about that. My own daddy, God rest his soul, always said they was nawthin more than killers."

"Like the greedy men who put them down in the black hell weren't killers? You're right, we should change the subject."

Each was silent as they watched the Rosses toss their litigation bags in to the back seat of their Mercedes. Mary smiled when Daniel Ross opened the car door for his wife. "It might be different in a lot of ways, Marge. But, ya know, chivalry ain't dead."

"Ellen Powell told me those two used to be enemies. She says they became friends the night the Kwikshop was robbed."

"That's something. What else did you hear happened?"

"Well, Beth Malley says she thought they were all going to die because of the way Emily and Daniel acted during the hold up. She don't know no more than that, she says. But Beth ain't much of a talker."

"Know what, Marge? I heard it was the robber who made them friends."

"Hmm. Wonder how that could be, Mary?"

Just here, Mary's husband, Will, asked, "You ladies gossiping again?"

"No hosey tonight, Will? Get on with ya. We've important things to talk out."

"On my way, dear wife. I was looking at CNN."

'Will, before you go . . . what do you know about the Rosses? Margaret says they were bitter enemies until the night young Tom Midnight robbed the store."

"Well, I'll be darned. Ya mean there's something about some one in this town that you two don't know?"

"Quit yer kidding. If ya know, tell us."

Will lit his pipe and sat down in the matching ladderback next to his wife. "And, let me tell you, ladies, this is fact."

🕮 . . .

Attorney Emily Malloy stopped in at the Kwikshop to buy fat-free milk for her morning coffee. With the milk, a quart bottle of juice and an armful of other grocery items, she approached the check-out clerk. She tried to keep her order from spilling onto the countertop but "Damn!" she let go aloud. "I'm terribly sorry." Juice ran across the floor. She knelt in this slippery mess and began collecting the shards of glass.

"Oh my God!" the clerk shot and then began to sob.

"Look, I said I'm . . ." Emily found herself looking down the barrel of the wavering pistol unsteadily trained on her by some lanky and trembling kid towering over the check-out clerk. He appeared scared. "You!" he shouted, at Emily. "Onto your feet! And drop that chunk of glass!"

Emily stood, slowly, her left hand still clutching a loaf of crumpled bread.

"Drop the hunka glass. That's a command!"

His facial features were distorted by the nylon stocking he wore stretched over his head. Despite his outward appearance, he was, Emily guessed, probably still in his teens and, moreover, nearly scared out of his wits.

"Get over here! Stand next to this counter!" Kid-the-Commander barked at Emily. "I'm keepin an eye on you!"

Backing toward the counter, Emily felt her knees weaken. She heard the clerk sob. Poor thing, she told herself while pitying the petite sales girl, not a day over sixteen. Was she holding down her job to earn spending money? Emily had used to do that. This girl's name tag read: "Beth." Emily knew that keeping calm could be the ticket to saving Beth's life and her own.

"Listen to me," Emily told her, while keeping her voice at an even pitch. "It'll be all right, Beth. Just do as he says."

Gunboy pivoted. "You! Over here!" he ordered, waving his pistol. "Now!"

Daniel James Ross walked up to the checkout counter and stood next to Emily. "If this isn't the way to end a perfectly rotten day. A hold up! In Sylvantia!" He dropped his groceries and threw up his arms, way over his head. "Fancy meeting you here, Ms. Malloy," he said. "I didn't think I ever would see YOU shopping at a convenience market. I thought your type would have hired help to handle such trivialities while you fight for truth and justice."

"And I can see that you, Mister Ross, remain an arrogant fool."

"Ah, well I do miss sparring in the courtroom. Though, I am certain, one day we shall have a go at it once again. I've abandoned criminal law and all that awfully ugly family nonsense. I see, however, that you've chosen to remain among those loyal to His Highness, the Duke of District Attorneys, the..."

"Do it again you say? Well, if we live through this present event, you have my word, Attorney Ross, that I will do what I did the last time we -- as you put it -- sparred. Once again, I shall kick your legal ass across the courtroom."

"Shut up, goddammit!" the boy with the pistol hollered. "I won't use this gun if I don't have to. But if I have to I will. You. Checker-girl. Empty this register."

"I . . . I have to ring a sale before it'll open."

"Here," Emily offered, "ring up my bread." She dropped the loaf of bread on the counter.

Daniel rolled his eyes. If there was a reason he was a chauvinist, Emily Malloy was it. "Other than helping rob this place, do you have any idea what you're doing?"

To her way of seeing things, Daniel Ross was as intolerable as she remembered from his days as a public defender in the Fairlane County Legal Services office. He was smart, all right, but he had lost out to her consistently on every case in the decade that they had dueled over cases involving domestic violence, child custody and abuse, as well as all the petty crimes that somehow managed to wend their way into the system and into the county court. Pompous, he also was spoiled. "You know, Daniel, if you'd think less about the past and more about how to help get us out of this mess, we'd all be better off for it."

"I ain't here ta listen to nobody fightin' about bullshit! Gimme that cash!"

Bad situation or not, Daniel could not resist another shot at his former adversary. "You mean you don't carry a gun, Emily? I thought for certain your type of woman would pack a piece. You know, if you only would put down the Constitution and pick up a copy of *Mademoiselle*, you might be mistaken for the most beautiful woman in this world."

"Shut the hell up!" the kid told Daniel. Shaking his head and exhaling, he fired a shot at the ceiling, causing plaster to rain downward onto the countertop. "I'll kill all of you if you don't goddamn get quiet!"

His threat brought fresh terror to Beth's face. Her legs gave way as she fainted. Her head struck the edge of the counter as she was on her way to the floor.

"Let'r go!" the kid shouted while looking at Emily. "Get in back the register and get me that money!"

Emily forced her legs to carry her around the meat cooler to the rear of the counter. Stepping over Beth to reach the cash register, she saw that the girl's forehead was bleeding. Emily's eyes met Daniel's.

Daniel recognized her plea. Of all the patently unfair choices one has to make in life. For him, it had come to this. He had no choice but to help her, the "devil woman."

Emily pulled $20 bills from the register drawer. "You think you're going to put all this in your pocket?" she asked Kid-the-Commander.

"What? Whadya care? Just give it to me."

"How old are you?"

"Hand me that money!" He raised the pistol, at her face.

Emily caught her breath. Was she doing the right thing? "Damn! I dropped the tens!"

"Get 'em!" the kid said. He jumped toward the counter. "No funny stuff down there on the floor, you," he said. "Hear me?" He moved closer toward the cash register, apparently forgetting that Daniel was now to his rear. "Maybe I should just blow off your head!"

What now, Emily thought. If Daniel had an opportunity, would he move to help them? Emily figured she was going to die. Don't think that way, she told herself. Give him some credit.

"Come on! Move it!" the kid said, visibly unnerved, his forehead dripping perspiration. "Are you deaf, you dumb bitch? I said I'll kill all of you!"

Emily remained silent. She could hear her heartbeat. Daniel had to know she was acting on a plan. He had to realize she was trying to get this kid to focus on her. Didn't he? If not, now what? Get up and hand him the money was the only choice.

Meanwhile, Daniel put his right foot in front of his left, careful not to step on any of the glass pieces on the floor. Just take one more step, and you have him, he told himself. Grab the arm with the gun, Daniel. Go!

Emily heard the gun fire. Her knees felt like jelly and her stomach churned. Why was it so quiet? Get up, Emily. Stand up, she urged herself.

"Ms. Malloy? You going to stay down there under cover or come up and help me subdue this boy?"

Emily forced her legs to work. As she rose over the counter, she saw Daniel, his left arm around the bandit's neck, his right hand holding the pistol.

"I'll call the ambulance and the police," she said. "This girl's head has a helluva gash in it."

"Right," Daniel replied. "I'll guard our hostage." He pulled off the robber's mask.

A boy of around eighteen looked upward at him. "It's all over now," he told Daniel.

"You're right. It is over. You're going to jail, where you belong."

In rushed two police officers followed by the ambulance crew. One of the cops took the gun from Daniel, handed it to her partner, cuffed the boy and read him his rights. Although the bandit's face was lowered by then, Emily had heard what this boy who but a few minutes earlier had threatened to kill her just now had said: "I'm sorry. Really, I am. I knew this was wrong, but it seemed like my only option, the only one I could figure on. I need to pay for my books at college."

Meanwhile, Officer Jennifer Rore had turned to ask Emily if there was anything she wanted to add to the police report, and Emily told her that Daniel's account had summed up the event in its entirety.

"That'll do for now, then. I'll contact you if I need anything further. You're both free to go," Rore said.

"Right," Daniel said. "Thanks. I'm ready for a Manhattan. Maybe two."

While taking her leave alone, Emily thought of ignoring Daniel's good work. Instead, however, she stopped and extended her hand to him. "Thank you, Daniel." Then she swung on her heels and headed toward the door.

"Ms. Malloy -- er -- Em? Emily? Would you care to join me at the Coal Street Café for a drink?"

"No, thank you. I am heading for the police station."

"Why ever for?"

"For this kid who could have killed us."

"What! But why?"

"You heard him as well as I heard him -- he was robbing this place to pay for textbooks."

"Oh, come on, Emily Malloy. Get off it, will you, please? You don't actually believe that line of crap, do you? What do you imagine he's studying in college for crying out loud: Robbery 101?

"You're crazier than him," Daniel told her. "How ludicrous, Malloy. I've never known you to think like a liberal. And why would YOU, of all people, believe him?"

"No state shall make or enforce any law which shall abridge the privileges or immunities of citizens of the United States: nor shall any State deprive any person of life, liberty or property, without due process of law; nor deny to any person within its jurisdiction the equal protection of the laws."

"Are you putting me on, or what, Malloy? How many criminals also know the Constitution and try to use it for their own devious ends? Eh? C'mon."

"How fast you have forgotten the little people, Daniel. What happened to your public defender attitude? Was it bought out?"

"I am not following you, Malloy. AND I think that remark was uncalled for."

"You're on the other side of midnight."

"What in hell are you talking about?"

"Midnight vs. Pennsylvania, Daniel. The case in which I prosecuted the man whom I know is this kid's father -- the one jailed for robbing the gas station over on South Main."

"Big deal! It obviously runs in the family." Daniel's eyes widened, "I do remember: the descendant of a Molly Maguire. His grandfather changed the family name to protect them from the stigma of their ancestor, didn't he?"

"Yes."

"Midnight told the judge that he wished for himself that he had received an education. He said he was paying for his ignorance because he was a lawless illiterate. He would do his time, he said. But, he wanted his boy to have what he hadn't. He didn't want him working in the black hell. All he wanted for his Tommy, he'd said, was for Tommy to have a real chance in life. Malloy, he was sincere. I remember that about him. That's why I fought so hard for him. And you . . . Well, you had a job to do, Malloy."

Emily nodded. "I remember that and more. I was accused of prosecuting one of my own. Remember? His great-granddaddy and mine were allies, so history says."

Daniel watched as she strode down the dimly-lit street, her purse slapping her hip. "Hey! Malloy? Wait! I'll come along with you."

With little light on their path, they walked beside each other, steadying the other's step as they crossed the railroad tracks.

✐ . . .

Will re-lit his pipe. "Ladies, that was the way of it. It makes ya think, ya know? If only the rest of the people in Fairlane made peace as well as the Rosses have."

"Ah go on with ya. Won't happen as long as people believe my people were born with murder in their hearts," Mary told him.

Book Two

Cait Beck

Ripple

Once while here with her little sisters, Cait caught a half dozen salamanders. Wet, muddy and happy, she took the creatures home and gave them refuge in a Holy Family Church carnival fish bowl she placed on the dresser in her bedroom. She had used the stripping pit water, rocks and moss she had pulled from the muddy banks to make the lizards, as she had called them, feel at home.

Days later, Cait received a tongue lashing from her mother because the slimy amphibians had escaped. Some time after that, her mother had found them shriveled and dead inside unworn shoes in Cait's closet.

In the way of organized recreation, there was not much for the children of campestral Ferndale to do. That meant nothing to Cait, who could find happiness in mud. Her father had taught her to use the bountiful natural resources of Fairlane County and the power of imagination as playtime tools. Cait had grown to love exploring the woodlands around her home.

✎ . . .

Sitting here now as an adult and remembering happy things about this place, Cait cried. Squinting in the reflection of sunlight on snow, she thought she saw him standing on the rocky promontory above her, and she jumped to her feet.

"Daddy?"

Her call echoed. One "daddy" became many carried on the nippy wind until all she heard was a dying "d." Cait blinked, and wiped tears from her cheeks. Nothing there. She blinked again. Still nothing.

Feeling like she was running toward a head-on crash with insanity, Cait screamed aloud. He was only hours dead. His body was still on a table in the Fairlane Hospital morgue. They were going to cut him open like students dissect the chest cavity of a frog in biology class. The thought made her stomach lurch.

If there were such a place as Heaven, he would be resting now after his fight with death, the only fight of his life that he had not won. He would check in with God and then rest up for spring gobbler season and the opening day of trout fishing. Wouldn't that be the case? Or would he be mad because his work was unfinished? He had never left a project undone.

She heard her own screams pierce the frosty February air. "No! No...no...o."

Her father had brought her to know the strippin', as these places were called. She well remembered her first sight of it. It was a day much warmer than this, a day much happier than this.

Holding his hand, she trudged over the dry creek bed and through brush and scrub oak until they reached the dusty old mining road. He was bringing her to pick huckleberries. Her mother would bake a pie -- the best huckleberry pie in all of Ferndale.

"Look, daddy! Look at the water! Oh, it's so pretty!"

"It's a strippin' pit," he said, half-smiling, half grimacing. "There's old mining shovels, and cars and all kinds of junk in the bottom of there," her father had said.

"Can ya swim in there, daddy?"

"Yea, Caitie, sure ya can," he had answered. "When you're bigger we'll do that."

They had sat on the edge of the pit then, letting their feet dangle in its water. As she pried pebbles from the water's edge, he had told her how men pulled hard coal out the earth to heat homes and fuel the industrial revolution many years before even he was born.

"That's how the pit got here. And then God filled it with water," he had said.

🙠 . . .

How long ago that was, Cait thought. How many fights had they had since that sweltering, summer evening when he held her hand and brought her here for the first time?

He had tried to marry her off to a young man whom Cait had found friendly but repulsively provincial. He had been against her going to college, believing that where she belonged was working in the factory on the hill or staying at home to raise children and care for a husband.

"I don't care how smart you are. I'm not spending money on college for a girl. You'll just end up married and having babies. That's what you all do. That's what you ought to do anyway," he had told her, and often.

Cait knew that he had loved her, of course, and she knew that he had been proud of her achievements. Although he had never been one to give voice to his heart, his approval showed in his actions toward her. He bought her motorcycles and guns and took long walks with her on weekend afternoons.

She laughed at her vision of him white-robed and wearing sandals. The man who did not wear suits? The man who at his father's funeral six months earlier stuffed his tie in his trouser pocket and his false teeth in the breast pocket of his blazer?

What kind of impression would he make on God? Cait laughed, remembering what her father had said during the Sign of Peace at her grandfather's funeral mass. "This is the part where they should stop Mass and let you go out to have a cigarette. Now, that's peace."

If the dead walked the earth, her father would come often to this place. He would come to see how the creek was flowing. Its pace meant the health of the trout he had stocked in the man-made dam they had built years ago in back of their home.

"I ain't crazy, yet," he had told Cait when they were knee-deep in silt and mud, making the breast of the kidney-shaped natural swimming pool. "You ain't crazy until you buy your own bulldozer."

Cait knew that she would have to go back. People were at his home, rushing to the side of his grieving girlfriend. Ferndale was in shock that Earl Beck was dead at 50. Only 12 hours ago, according to the neighbor, he had been in O'Donnell's Sporting Goods, drinking coffee and talking with the guys.

Only two decades ago, he was holding her hand and talking about strippin' pits. Only nine years ago, he was at her high school graduation in Clarion, looking like a proud daddy. Only three years ago, he was holding Cait's daughter, his granddaughter. And, today . . . today, he was dead.

Cait pried a pebble from the frozen soil and threw it into the water. In the wavelet that formed, she thought she saw his rounded face and the blue of his eyes.

Meanwhile, back at Beck's house, his mother was bemoaning Cait's lack of manners. She had already been out by the creek to see if her granddaughter was there.

"I'll tell you," she said, wagging a finger, "Earl will never be dead so long as that one is alive. There are important things to be done. There's a house full of company. And where is she? Off in the woods. Off in her own head."

Above, at the strippin', Cait buried her hands in her pockets and breathed deeply of the snowy air. "Oh, I know you're here, Dad. So let's go watch the show, eh?"

Autumnal Awakening

During early childhood, Cait Beck had spent untold hours of her free time here, in the garret, on the third floor of her grandmother's house.

Presently thirty-two and ascending the stairs leading to the attic (as others would call it), Cait felt a flutter of excitement in her heart. It was the same happy feeling that overwhelmed her when she used to come up here to write her "storybooks," which were compositions she had begun while in the second grade at Holy Cross Elementary School in Ferndale.

The noon angelus sounding from the tower at the Saint Francis Holy Roman Catholic Church filled her with a sense of security. It was another of the few happy things she recalled from childhood.

Life once had gone less perfectly than Cait had wished, her happiness having been annihilated by her parents' divorce. They were the first couple to divorce in Ferndale. Catholic parents raising three Catholic school daughters did not do that sort of thing. It was mortal sin, worse even than marrying a non-Catholic.

That single catastrophe, the divorce, had given rise to three assumptions that Cait carried like a crucifix. First: Someone was bad; second, Life was a nightmare from which one never awakened until after death; and third, All happiness longed for never would be realized. Happiness couldn't be found no matter how many Rosaries she prayed while in the dark of her bedroom on lonely nights spent alone while living at home with her mother. Her heart had felt about ready to burst from sorrow and from fear.

Cait's weekend afternoon tea parties spent here in this attic had been over long before they should have been. She no longer had "to act" the part of a grown-up. Instead, she was expected to behave as one after being forced into the role of surrogate adult; and this, years before her body would sprout breasts and pubic hair. Like being made to swallow a bitter medicine meant to cure a nagging cough, the experience of raising two "baby sisters," cooking, and taking care of household chores never seemed beneficial. So, weekend visits to her grandparents', and her escape into her imagination while at play in this attic had provided her with comfort.

🖋 . . .

Cait walked into the front room, where the old brass beds looked as comfortable as they once had been to her so long ago. Cait recalled those nights when she lay snuggled beneath the gold-and-white quilt, while she and her Nana, Mary Elizabeth, her paternal grandmother, had slept together there "close to the stars," as they had liked to agree between them.
The old traveler's trunk, her grandmother's grip, now was covered with dust. Without looking, she knew that

brightly colored dresses, beads, wire-rimmed "granny glasses," thick-soled and worn black leather boots, and babushkas still would be inside.

The trunk had a flat top that had made for an excellent table. On it, Cait had served her "tea" and "cakes," which were Nana's fresh-brewed iced tea and Oreos or Vienna Fingers, which ever was in the Currier and Ives cookie tin in the kitchen.

Now, as it had been back then, the floor boards creaked as she crossed the room toward the armoire, or "Cait's closet", as her Nana used to call it. She pulled opened its doors and looked in on her grandmother's tributes to fashion. Smiling, she took out a brilliant-yellow, beaded purse, wherein she found a pair of elbow-length white gloves tinted yellow by time. While pushing the purse up her left forearm, she pulled one of the gloves onto her right hand. *Fits much better than when you were five.* From on the shelf, she pulled down a broad-rimmed, canary yellow straw hat and plopped it on top of her head. Then she pulled on the other glove, while she pranced toward a beveled mirror. *No need to get onto tip-toes now to see me.*

While she was standing there dressed in these old playthings, the voice of a happy little girl filled her thoughts. *"Oh! Princess!*

You silly girl! Shall we take tea? Come, let's pour our tea here atop our table. Careful now, this is Nana's best china!"

Princess, her grandfather's shorthair spaniel, had died fourteen years ago. Pop, Cait's grandfather, had bought Princess to hunt pheasants in the fall and to go along with him when he went fishing for trout in the spring. No hunting dog at heart, Princess tracked adventure here with the fair-skinned, chubby, bookish girl who always had time to play at a game of fetch the stick.

Just as she had done as a girl, Cait seated herself on the attic floor with her back leaned against the armoire. She drew her knees in toward her chest. Tears welled in her eyes. She felt such a dire sense of loss. But why? Her Nana's poor physical and mental condition? Perhaps. Or was it her own selfishness causing her to feel this way? Perhaps it, too. "After all," she told herself, "you're a grown woman of thirty-two now, Cait. Gone are your halcyon days of unadulterated innocence, lazy, dream-like days once lived in a world of make-believe unfettered by routine." *Gone, too, is the enchantment once present in this attic, where you used to sing to yourself, and write your stories in which imaginary people listened to you and understood you. Soon, Nan will be gone. What then?*

Beams of late-morning sunshine burst through the east window. Cait watched this light grow brighter. The sunlight cast across the floor was just as it had been back when she was five years old. Not a thing about this room had changed, really. Only the times had changed. And, so too, the people who once had inhabited it also had changed: she and her grandmother.

Cait knew that if she ventured over to the window her eyes would feast on the forested mountainside in full September splendor. She did not want to get up and go back downstairs, to her grandmother. She wanted to stay on a while longer in this musty room, to go on admiring these relics, remembrances of a time past. She wanted to go on reviving memories of a less-complicated time in her life, and also of the special kind of happiness that neither she nor any other grown woman would, or could, or probably should, expect to know ever again. Those early girlhood days had been lived with a purity of heart. She had believed that all people were good, that all of life was a wonderful, happy adventure --- just like in her "storybooks," and that she would get everything and more of what she wanted and deserved for herself. Then, the divorce happened.

Reality was the tightrope on which Cait had spent years balancing, sometimes not all that skillfully. What a melancholy mood came over her, after she pictured herself as an acrobat on a high-wire to which she could see no end. How unproductive these thoughts, she told herself, and abandoned this stance.

Like a sunflower while wearing the huge yellow hat, she stood momentarily before her image in the mirror. *So what? So what if things hadn't gone as planned in the unworldly mind of a little girl growing up in a provincial and protected place? You have so far made the best of your life. It has been an adventure.*

Her eyes caught sight of the item she had been sent up here to fetch for her grandmother — "the light-brown suitcase." Back in the days of dress up, this was Cait's "briefcase." She knelt before it now, while she pushed on the latches. And then — still there after all these years — her "storybooks," many of which were based on yarns about "the good old days."

Bound with construction paper, her manuscripts, the inside pages, although yellowed by age, were intact. Clutching these compositions to her breast, Cait felt as though she could dance a jig. She would take these stories along with her, home, to her daughter. These stitched-up patchworks of recollections of life as it once had been lived were so much more to Cait than mere souvenirs. These "storybooks" were proof to her that there had been one dream she acted upon long before her time ran out.

Cait tossed the straw hat and the beaded purse into the armoire, just as she had done as a girl. She grabbed her grandmother's suitcase and skipped toward the stairway. At the head of the steps, she halted to make a mental image of this attic. Her eyes focused on a sunbeam. She exhaled a deep breath. She had captured the enchantment of the dream of dreams once dreamt here while she still had been a small girl on a visit to this place.

🐌 . . .

Downstairs now, Cait saw her grandmother in the living room, lying in her recliner as she did so often these days, her hands clasped over her breastbone, her eyelids opened wide and her eyes gazing at the plaster ceiling. She had given up — resigned herself to death. The only thing left to do was wait until Jesus picked her number. The wait would not be long, she often told Cait and any one else who would listen.

Her chamber pot, a 10-gallon, enamel stock pot with lid, remained in the corner at the far end of the room, away from any of the three windows. Her grandmother once had told her that when she was growing up there were no bathrooms in houses. Everyone in Store Patch had had a chamber pot in their bedroom. "Was a lot better than goin' outside in the snow to the outhouse, to pee."

"What in hell were you doing up there so long? Did you find it?" Her eyes remained anchored to the ceiling.

"Yes, Nan." Dutifully on her way to handing over her grandmother's suitcase, Cait felt torn between a deep sense of sorrow and another of deep relief. By then, she had seated herself on her grandmother's couch. "Guess what else? My stories! What a surprise!"

"Stories? What stories you talkin' about, Sherri?"

"Nana? I'm Cait." She would have chalked up her grandmother's confusion between she and her cousin to old age if she had not been called Sherri on many occasions in her life. Nan always had muddled their names. Cait and Sherri, who was three years older and the first-born grandchild, always laughed about it. So too did Lauren, Sherri's sister, and Marissa, Cait's sister, whose names their Nana had also confused on a regular basis.

"My stories. Don't you remember, Nan? When I was little and played in the garret for hours on end? Remember me always pestering you for more paper? Remember your yarns? I'll take them and knit them into *real* books now?"

"Nope," her grandmother grumbled. "Don't remember. Don't remember nothin' nomore."

"They were all inside your suitcase, Nan. The one you sent me to the garret for. What a great find!"

"Oh, well, if it means *that* much to ya, then ya can have it."

"Have what, Nan? My stories? Well, of course . . ."

Mary Elizabeth slammed the recliner handle and her upper body sprang to a sitting position. "The suitcase, ya dummy, you," she said to Cait. "There's more suitcases up the garret, ain't they?"

"Well, yes. But you had said you wanted your suitcase. I guess I was surprised to find my stories in there. I'd thought you'd taken this suitcase along with you to Ireland a few years back."

"What are ya talkin about? Ireland? Such silliness, Sherri. Just take the suitcase and go get me another. Then pack up that pile of clothes for me. And *don't* be all day about it." Mary Elizabeth pushed herself back to the reclining position and re-affixed her eyes to the ceiling.

What might she be thinking whenever she lay there waiting "for Jesus to pick her number"? Was she envisioning Heaven? Was she reliving her life? Was she regretting the dreams she had forfeited to raise her sons here in rural Store Patch as compared to so doing in Fairlane Junction with its department stores and rail cars and busy streets?

Cait had grown accustomed to her grandmother's strange state-of-mind. Mary Elizabeth had been slowly shutting the door on reality for some time. Growing used to something, though, is quite different from accepting it. Cait was having a hard time believing that this house, a symbol of security, would no longer be theirs. That she would not be able to run in the front door and find Mary Elizabeth standing before the stove, cooking up a batch of mashed potatoes and brewing fresh tea.

🕊 . . .

Although she had placed her construction paper storybooks on the coffee table to read as time allowed, it was days before Cait had the opportunity to even glance at them, even in passing on her way out the door. She had been walking the highwire, again. This time, though, she had seen the end of the line and safely dismounted.

Her Nana was safe now. Safe, though utterly hostile at times. The resentfulness did not sway Cait's belief that they had done the right thing. Still, her grandmother's behavior was not always easy to tolerate. On days when her patience wore thin, Cait would abandon Mary Elizabeth's room to take a walk outside, where she could have a good cry. "I am not going to sit here and listen to you feel sorry for yourself," Cait would holler and throw her arms up in the air.

So, having made peace with herself, while in her own kitchen and looking out the windows as the last of the crumbling, colored leaves flitted to the ground, Cait picked up her construction paper storybooks.

Were there words in any of these worth saving? How had her young mind conceived to sign and date each one? What could ... The ringing of the telephone interrupted her thoughts.

"I'm sorry's all I want to say," her grandmother said in a voice that bore the weight of her torment.

"That's okay, Nana." It was okay. Wasn't it? Nana hadn't intended to be *that* hateful toward her earlier. Had she?

"I forget, some. But, I'm okay now. I just don't want ya to be mad at me is all."

What should I say? Cait was trying to understand. She was laboring to deal with the changes in this old woman's life, changes that forced change on Cait. Even the matriarch's telephone number had changed when she went to the nursing home. Yes, Mary Elizabeth Beck finally had made it out of Store Patch and into Fairlane Junction, although not as she once had intended. Not as a young woman bursting with will and ambition, but as an old woman, suffering dementia. Cait found difficulty committing her grandmother's new telephone number to memory. Try as she did to remember, the seven digits refused to register. Cait had to record it in her daily calendar and on handwritten notes stuck to the walls by her telephones.

Having accepted that she no longer was competent to live at home alone, Mary Elizabeth had made the decision herself, "to go into the nursin' home." After all, what was there at home? The cook stove. The quiet. The oil burner. The quiet. The grocery list. The quiet. The snow. The quiet. The stairs. And, the loneliness; and this, no matter how many times someone telephoned or dropped in for a visit.

"I'm not angry with you, Nan. I was, but so were you. It's all right."

"Sometimes I'm angry at the world," Mary Elizabeth confided, then giggled like a school girl.

Suddenly, on that declaration, Cait knew the depth of her grandmother's anguish.

"Ya there, Cait?"

"Yes. Yes, I am, Nana. And I always will be, even when you're angry."

"Tomorrow, I might be angry all over again. I love ya, though. Ya should remember that, Cait."

"I love you, too, Nana." *I love you even though you're old and forgetful and, sometimes, nasty. I love you in spite of your limitations. I love you even though you can't take care of yourself anymore. I love you even though the fire has gone out of your spirit and the sparkle in your eyes is but a twinkle.*

"Well, good. So long as you ain't angry at me. Why did I hang up on ya anyway? I don't remember. Can't. Not anymore."

"What does it matter? You were angry is all. Don't worry about it, Nana. Just get rest and stay healthy."

"Healthy? C'mon, Cait. Health ain't gonna happen, not for me. It's old age, ya know. I'm fadin'. Gonna be like that some days. I get the maddest when I can't recall a single soul and when I cannot remember things about the good old days."

"If it makes you feel any better, Nana, don't ever forget that I know all of your stories, because you've told them to me. You know that I know your stories, don't you?" *But for how long will you know?*

"I guess. Well, I'm keepin' ya too long."

"Take care, Nan. Please don't worry about things."

Back to sitting quietly with her stories, Cait relived snippets of her childhood. In mind, she was transported back to Mary Elizabeth's back yard, where, more than twenty years ago, each April, she "picked" great bunches of lilacs. She had captured the essence of this springtime ritual in a story, "Lilac Mornings."

Nana knits, swaying in the creaky, wooden rocker on the back porch. I know that she is watching me pick the purple flowers that make her smile. I know because even though her face is downward, toward her afghan, I can see her smile. She doesn't smile lots. That's why I like to pick her lilacs. So I can see her be happy.

⁂ . . .

"Hi Mommy." Her face, Cait's daughter's, wore the tidings of a happy heart.

"Hi Emmy."

In ran Emily, her overstuffed backpack dangling from her arm. Off went the shoes, Down went the lunch box. "Whacha doin?"

Cait hugged her daughter and planted a kiss on her forehead. "Hi, darling. How was school?"

"Okay, except Thomas Rierdon is yucky."

"Why is Thomas yucky?" She knew the Rierdon boy to be a pleasant little fellow. Emily had introduced him one afternoon when he and his mother showed up at the playground. He and Emily played for hours on the swings and the teeter-totter.

"He teases me, Mom."

"Oh well, then he must like you very much. Boys tease the object of their affections, you know." Cait stifled a laugh.

"Yuck!" Emily bounced in to the kitchen and opened the refrigerator. "I like those stories, Mom. I read some of them the other day, when you went out for a walk. Why'd ya write them?"

"Because no little boys teased me. Because I didn't have the Internet to occupy hours of my time when I was a little girl. Because I really liked to play in your great Nana's garret."

Emily sat at the kitchen table. Dunking an Oreo in a glass of milk she asked, 'What do ya mean ya didn't have the Internet?"

"Emily, there was no Internet when I was your age. At least not for citizens to use. The government had some form of it."

"Boring! Hey, when you were little you wrote lots, and you grew up to be a writer. Does that mean since I play school all the time that I'll grow up to be a teacher?"

It was true. Emily often instructed her dolls and stuffed animals. Cait would listen to her drilling math facts and spelling words into Molly, Josephina and Kristy, Emily's dolls.

"You can grow up to be anything you want to be. If you're thinking on being a teacher, great. You'll have had lots of practice, right?"

"Yea, I guess, Mom." She concurrently crammed an entire Oreo in her mouth and talked. "Why did you play in Nana's attic? It stinks up there."

How different she is from me when I was little, Cait thought. Different, and yet, the same. "Oh, the garret was magical to me. It was the neatest place in Nan's house. Maybe the coolest place in the whole world."

"Like my bedroom is to me?"

"Yes, like your bedroom is to you." Cait stacked the story books, running a finger over the crinkled edge on the cover of the top manuscript. "Listen, Emily, you may have these if you want them."

Emily wiped her mouth with her forearm and chugged down the last sips of milk and soggy cookie pieces. "Hey, cool. I can use them in my pretend English class. I'm gonna go play school right now."

"Here you go then," Cait said, handing the pile of stories to Emily. "Let me know how your students like them."

Despite that she truly wanted Emily to have the stories, Cait also felt a pang of remorse at handing them over. She didn't know why.

"Thanks, Mommy. I'll take good care of them."

Cait smiled, feeling grateful. So Emily had sensed her mother's brief, unspoken reluctance. Emily understood.

"I don't like giving away Christmas presents after I buy them for people," Emily confided. "I don't know why, Mommy, but I don't. Some, I think, are too pretty to give away. I want them for my own."

The child's awareness was more than keen, Cait judged. "Come here. Give me a hug. Now off you go. Give lots of homework. And, make sure you do your own homework. Your REAL homework."

Cait went to her office, which was next to Emily's bedroom. She touched the mouse to deactivate her screensaver and read the last paragraph of the story she was writing.

"I'll get it," Emily yelled, running down the hall toward the telephone.

"It's Great Nana, Mommy."

Cait lifted the receiver in her office. "What's up, Nan. You forget something?"

"Where the hell is my suitcase?"

"What?" Cait heard Emily hang up the other line. She didn't blame her.

"My light brown suitcase. The one you were supposed to put my clothes in. It ain't here. I looked in the closet. I looked under this bed."

"You gave it to me weeks ago, Nana. Remember? I packed your things in the big navy case. After we unpacked your clothes at your new place, I put the case in the closet."

"I know. I know. That one's there. Where's my light-brown suitcase?"

"I just told you. You gave it to me."

"Why in hell would I give you MY suitcase. I ain't dead yet."

"Who said anything about being dead? You gave it to me."

"No, I didn't. I want it. You bring it to me, do you hear? You get it down here."

"Okay. Okay. Calm down, Nan. I'll bring it down on the weekend."

"Well, you'd better."

"I . . ." Mary Elizabeth slammed down the telephone.

Cait gently replaced her receiver as Emily burst in to the room. Wow! Mommy, what's she so mad about?"

"Ah, don't worry about it, Emily. She's old and she forgets."

Emily wore a quizzical expression. She rocked from side to side and raised one of Cait's manuscripts to look at it. "Mom?"

"Huh?"

"Do ya want your stories back?"

Cait turned toward her daughter and beckoned her to come for a hug. "No, darling, you keep them. I shall write new ones."

Dress Rehearsal

The whole town is ready to party because Maggie Dougherty died last night.

The old Irish lady had lived her every day in Store Patch, a village of 600, including the dogs. Tiny as it is, the village is not without services for its people. There are three barrooms and a church in Store Patch. The taprooms are on the lower road. The church sits on the high road. It is common knowledge that before you can go the bar, you must go to church wearing your Sunday best, and a smile. Even if your pew mate is your fiercest enemy, you must offer the sign of peace when Father O'Malley directs.

Maggie was a well-known and well-liked old lady. She never missed Sunday Mass. She belonged to the hosey auxiliary and, in her younger old days, she was a visitor to shut-ins. She also gave out the best Halloween candy and grew strawberries in her garden for all the kids in the neighborhood.

So, to give her a proper send-off, many of the old Irish women in Store Patch are cookin' and buyin' spirits for her wake.

☙ . . .

My grandmother, whom I call "Nana," called me earlier this morning to tell me this news. Actually, her call was a subtle way of letting me know that she wanted me here, with her. Naturally, I obliged.

"Dis is nawthin', Caitie. When I was little, I remember mom and pop wakin' da neighbor's husband ... Cluny... yep... old Cluny Fagin ... Oh my, whatatime," my grandmother says.

"Right in the house?"

"Yes, of course, in the house. There were no funeral homes back then. At Cluny's wake, the women folk gathered round the coffin. It was set up on an old kitchen table in the middle of the parlor. Mind ya, the men were in the kitchen, drinking shots of boilo and telling stories about Cluny. They said he would hold his liquor better than any 10 Irishmen and any 50 Lithuanians."

"Was it the booze that killed Cluny?"

"No. He died in a mine accident, Cait. That was the usual cause of death for men back then, ya know. Not that drink didn't kill a lot of 'em who survived the mines to spend their nights and weekends in the pub. Anyway, Mrs. Fagin, I think her name was Caileen, was kneeling before the body of Cluny. And, everybody knew, ya see, that there was no love lost in that marriage. Cluny was a drunk, a womanizing, good-fer-nawthin' bum. And, Caileen, bless her, well she was a Saint, and a beautiful one at that.

Nana sprinkles flour on the table and begins to knead the dough. "So, Caileen, not a tear in her eye, said good-bye to Cluny. She said, 'They be buryin' yiz face down, Cluny, my love, so that yiz be headed in the right direction.'"

"That's too funny," I say.

Nana, who had been very serious in the telling of her recollection sees nothing funny about it. I can tell by the fire in her eyes. She wipes flour from her nose.

Her contribution to the wake food will be soda bread and a heaping pot of ham, cabbage and potatoes. As far as I am concerned, there isn't a woman in all of Fairlane County who can make ham and cabbage as good as MY Nana. It's just a pity that somebody has to die before she cooks up a batch.

"Mind ya, the other women nodded approval of Caileen's partin' words to her husband. When Caileen left the coffin and joined her friends, they tipped their glasses to old Cluny and went on celabratin' in to the wee hours of the mornin.' I remember listenin' to 'em after Mother had sent me upstairs ta bed."

"You stayed in that house? With a dead person?"

"Everybody did."

Intrigued by the story and Nana's animated telling of it, I dig in the silverware drawer for a potato peeler. I might as well help while I listen.

"Nana, aren't the women supposed to keen at wakes? In Leon Uris' "Trinity" they do, and Uris is known for good research."

"Not today they don't. A few tears maybe, but nawthin' like when I was a girl."

"Well, why all this cooking if they don't do wakes in houses anymore?"

Nana covers her dough with a tea cloth. She pours herself a cup of tea and sits down at the table to help me peel the potatoes. Nana wears the countenance of a woman with a story on her lips.

"In the old days, travel was the reason. People had to come pretty far to attend a funeral. Didn't have good roads. Didn't have cars. Now, I suppose it's 'cause the family of the dead is too busy grieving to be cooking. Plus, other relatives and friends call on their house at all hours. There has to be food for all the company. Somebody's gotta cook it. I guess it's a way of being neighborly, a way of letting the family know they have your sympathy."

"Some one is knocking at the door, Nana," I say, but she is not hearing me. "You going to answer that, Nan?" Her body is rigidly still, potato peeler in her right hand, potato encircled in her left. Her eyes, kindled, are focused on something miles in the past.

"Okay then, I'll get it," I answer my own question.

Through the glass panes in the oak door, I looked into the eyes of Elaine O'Reilly.

"Hello, Caitie," she drawls on her way in to Nana's parlor, "'tis a sad, sad day for Store Patch. Who'da thunk we'd be payin' last respects to Maggie Dougherty? I thought the old lass 'ud be dancin' on our graves . . . Ah Marybeth," Elaine says upon seeing her lifelong girlfriend. "I suppose you're a busy one today."

I follow Mrs. O'Reilly into the kitchen, noticing that the visitor is overdressed for a Tuesday morning. It isn't check day and Father O'Malley finished parish visitation weeks ago. It must be because of Maggie, I think, eyeing Mrs. O'Reilly's black suit.

"Indeed, Elaine. I can hardly believe it meself," Nana says, and in the same breath, she issues marching orders to me. "Get Mrs. O'Reilly a cup of tea, dear. Me old legs need a rest."

Mrs. O'Reilly sits in my chair and starts working on the half-peeled potato I had abandoned to answer the door.

I watch them peel in silence. Their hands move fast and efficiently. *Will I ever become that skilled at spuds? How many hundreds, maybe thousands, of pounds of potatoes have their combined hands peeled?*

"Do ya think, Marybeth, that Maggie left all her money to the church like she said she was gointa on account of her no-good kids?"

"Sure, and the Virgin's comin' ta dinner, Elaine. Jesus, Mary and Joseph, yiz ought to wake up and smell the coffee."

I serve Elaine's tea and refresh Nana's cup.

"Maggie only said those things to keep the kids in line," Nana explains, potato peeler shaking at Elaine. "Mind ya, she left plenty for the church. Plenty. She had the money did Maggie. Never went nowhere. Never spent."

"I've already been to see the family," Elaine confides. "That's why I'm dressed. Normally, I'd be in the garden before the heat of the day comes on. I took 'em a meat-n-cheese tray."

"You was nosin is all," Nana says, adding a giggle. "A meat tray? Lordee. I'll be. I s'pose you din't make it yourself?"

"I ordered it from McNulty's, for cryin' out loud. It's too sunny and going to be too hot to fuss over a stove. Besides, it's not like it used to be. You're one of the last in town to bother so when somebody dies."

"I most certainly am not. Why Anna Marie Shay called earlier to see whether I wanted to go in on a bottle for the family. And, I know for a fact that Mary Theresa is baking. Besides, Caitie here is learnin' howta do this stuff so she can host my send-off. I hope its grand."

I almost lose my grip on Nana's teapot. "You want me to do this for you? You actually want me to do this when you die?"

"Certainly." Nana knives a potato in half with one whack. "Be only fittin'."

"Fitting for what, Nan? Even you said it's not the way it used to be."

"No. But Maggie's kids are doin' it fer her. It's what she wanted. And, it's what I want."

"Marybeth, they ain't wakin Maggie in her livin room," Elaine points out.

"Eejit! Who said anything about bein put out in my parlor?" Whack.

I am puzzled. "Well, if you aren't talking about that, what are you talking about then?"

"Cookin, for crying out loud! I don't want no meat and cheese platters on this table when people come to see you after I die." Whack.

I breath a sigh of relief. Somehow, I cannot see me playing Mrs. Politawicz, the mortician. Just going up to a casket at wakes makes me queasy. There is no way I could prepare my dead grandmother for viewing. Not for anything.

"Marybeth, what will you care? You'll be in Heaven with the Good Lord. Besides, today most don't even do funeral dinners. You ought to know this enough. A lot of our friends are dead. Their kids throw funeral breakfasts. They only do one or two drinks before and after the wake and the funeral.

Life goes on, ya know. Can't let death stop American production." Elaine heads to the sink to wash her starchy hands.

"Alls I know is if you both were helping with these taters, I could get a little rest before the activity," Nana counters. She was not to be bested, especially not by Elaine, lifelong friend or not.

"I have to run, dear. I want to go up to the rectory for a Mass Card. I'll see you at Maggie's this evening?"

"Fine. Be off with ya then. Caitie will help me."

"Actually, Nan, I must be off, too. American production, you know. I'll come back around 5 o'clock."

"Make sure ya do. Wear something presentable, too, you hear?"

"Something funereal, say."

Whack. "Something proper for wakin'. No short skirts. Something long and black." Whack. "And loose."

🖋 . . .

Mary Elizabeth spends the rest of the morning and part of the early afternoon cooking the ham and cabbage and baking her prize-winning bread. Opting for a bit of a rest before getting dressed to go, she goes to the living room, she reaches under the sofa cushion and pulls out her "black tablet."

Cait has been shown where it is. She has received serious instructions that she is not to read it until Mary Elizabeth is dead. "Not until ya see my soul float off to Heaven are ya to open this," she has repeatedly told her granddaughter.

"What's in it?" Cait asked the first time she saw her grandmother furiously scribbling in the tablet.

"Never you mind. Yiz'll find out soon enough."

Sitting back in her recliner, Mary Elizabeth chews on the BIC pen cap. She is organizing her thoughts to put on paper. She will have to provide all the details so the kids will do it all the right way.

She writes, "You are to prepare a big batch (10-gallon pot) of ham, cabbage and potatoes. Cait will know how. I told her how on the day Maggie Dougherty died. She actually helped me do the potatoes. Just in case she forgets though, I am writing down the recipe here. Buy the ham from McNulty's. A real ham. No pre-sliced trash."

The preparations tire her. There are so many things to remember. Mary Elizabeth falls soundly to sleep while writing out the recipe.

The tablet is filled with instructions. She has listed detailed details about buying sanctuary lights. She has placed $50 in an envelope and stapled it to the page on which she had written the directions for approaching the priest about the candles. "Spend the whole fifty on 'em." She has ordered no organ playing. "Bagpipers. Piping 'Amazin' Grace'."

☙ . . .

Nana is standing at the front door, stomping her foot when I arrive.

"What?"

"What? What indeed! It's 10 after is what. We have to get this food to the Dougherty's. They'll be leavin soon for the funeral home." She eyes me from head to toe. "Well, at least you dressed right."

"I had to go out and buy this today after I left," I tell her, running my hands along the long, black linen skirt. It is severe. No buttons. No show of legs. "I feel like a widow."

"Nonsense. It's lovely. Make sure you wear it to my event."

"What?"

"You heard me."

🐚 . . .

The food in the Dougherty house spills over from the kitchen into the living room, and from there, into the formal parlor. I calculate that more than a quarter of the residents of Store Patch are crammed into the room. They buzz and munch and drink down glassfuls of what looks like whiskey. My stomach burns.

"Marybeth and Cait. Oh, thank you, thank you so much for coming by." Margaret, Maggie's eldest daughter embraces us. "Mother would have been pleased."

"She was a great lady. A grand woman. I'll miss her," Nana says.

I feel awkward. I don't like this one bit. It's morose, to say the least.

"I made some things. Put 'em on the stove on low heat. There'll be plenty of hot food for the company when they come back after the wake," Nana tells Margaret.

"Thank you, dear Marybeth. And, thank you, Cait. For coming. I remember you when you were a baby. My how you've grown. You're a lovely woman."

I smile. What can I say to fill the embarrassing silence? What am I expected to say? "I . . . I'm sorry about Maggie. I'll always remember her."

"Thank you, Cait. Please help yourselves to a drink. We'll be off to the funeral home shortly."

There isn't a teetotaler in the place. Maggie's kitchen table looks like a buffet. Fifths of whiskey and gin and vodka and bottles of wine, red, white and pink, are uncapped and sitting on the table with plates of finger food. I spot Elaine's meat and cheese tray.

"Caitie, ya must make sure there's Seagram's on my table. And Seven-Up to go with it. And, please make sure you have plenty of ice." Nana pours a shot of Seagram's in to a glass and drinks it down like a miner just off his shift.

I watch her pour a second and drink it just as quickly. "You're going to mess up your medication if you keep pounding shots like that."

"Mind yer biznis, lassie. This is an important event for you. Give me a cigarette."

I know better than to argue. So, I open my purse, take out a cigarette and lighter and hand these to her.

'We're goin' to the parlor. We'll make sure we're seen and then leave for the funeral home. Follow me. Make sure you watch how it's done."

"How what's done?"

"How Margaret, sad or not, makes sure that the guests have enough to eat and drink and that talk is flowing easily."

The only thing flowing around here is booze and gossip. I think my Nana is losing her mind, but if I hadn't gotten the hint earlier, I have it now. I am in school. "Waking 101." I'd rather be home scrubbing the toilet bowel, to be honest. "You don't even begin to think that I can play hostess when you die. Do you?"

"Course I do, Caitie. And you'll do a fine job of it. Just keep your mouth shut and watch. Don't worry, there's time. You'll get the hang of it after a coupla these with me. John Cassidy tells me his mother is going out any day now. Then, there's old Francis James Laughlin. Too dumb to die I think, but it'll happen. I hope sooner than later."

☙ . . .

I stand behind Nana, who slipped in to a folding chair besides Mrs. O'Reardon, a fragile woman with whom she some times plays pinochle. They squeeze each other's hand like two school girls and Nana leans over and whispers to Mrs. O'Reardon. I can't hear what she says, but I assume it has something or another to do with me because Mrs. O'Reardon giggles and unsuccessfully sneaks a peak at me.

"A toast to Maggie," says Connor Cassidy, "a true lady, a true friend." Every body lifts a glass. I join them. My wine goes down like a tonic. "We'll miss her, for sure," Connor adds.

I have never before seen the likes of this at a funeral. In my mind, the very word makes me feel like crying. Hell, I've said good-bye to a lot of people, but funerals are so . . . permanent. Even when you part ways with a person, you know the individual is still around, even if he is creating misery for others. At least, it isn't death, even if there is a moment when that person makes you so miserable that you wish he were dead. How can they possibly laugh like they are at a party?

"T'is a grand wake. Maggie would have loved it," says her son, Francis. "Even in death, she is surrounded by good friends, good food, good banter. Drink up, friends. After Father O'Malley comes for a prayer, we will be off to the funeral parlor."

Why, I wonder, does Father come to the house if the body is at the funeral parlor? Friendship? Tithe? A glass of homemade dandelion wine?

"Jesus, Mary and Joseph, can yiz believe they buried Kennedy Jr. at sea? A good Catholic? At sea? Cremated, no less," bellows Scotty Feeley. "Why I was shocked. Not that I thought he shuda been buried at Arlington, mind ya, but, well the sea?"

I want to tell him that cremation is "back to ashes," just like Father says when he puts the black cross on our foreheads on Ash Wednesday. I want to tell him that cremation makes good land use sense. Don't cemeteries contribute to urban sprawl? Not that we have such a problem in Fairlane County.

"They just didn't want a parade at the Cathedral is what I think," Cliona Connelly says. "Millions woulda come, yiz know, to see him. Better to avoid such a display."

"Righto! Hell, there's plenty of our people at the bottom of the ocean, anyways. Those that died on them coffin ships were thrown overboard, I'm told," adds Patrick "Paddy" Boyle. "Watery grave, wormy grave, makes no difference, really. You're dead."

"No showing means lack of closure. Family can't grieve," my Nana argues. "Look at my Earl. None of us got to really say good-bye."

She's talking about my daddy, who was cremated. It was his wish. Fervent wish. To make sure that he got his way, Daddy carried a cremation card with him and pulled it out to show every one at family gatherings, including his father's funeral. Nana was against it from the start. Not that this stopped MY dad.

You make damn sure that this is what happens when I die, youse hear me?"

"Uhoh, dad's got his 'I want to be incinerated' ID out again," was the joke among his daughters. It wasn't a joke when he died young and suddenly. None of us got to say good-bye before they "incinerated" him.

My eyes fill with tears.

"Ah, Cait," Mrs. O'Reardon says, "Maggie lived a long, happy life. There's nawthin' ta cry about. Dry yer tears and have a lil' nip."

"Enough of this gloomy talk," Francis hollers. "There, I see Father walkin' up the steps now. Let's say a prayer and be on our way."

🕿 . . .

Nana is quiet on our short drive to Politawicz Funeral Home in Ferndale. I am not in the mood for banter either. I just want this shindig, for that's what it seems to me, to be over. I want to go home and forget all this. Mortality frightens me.

Just before leaving Maggie's house, Father blessed us and we prayed the *Our Father*. Every head in the place was bowed. Every mouth, previously exchanging quips and conversation about everything from Maggie's life to the upcoming presidential election, was now silent. Their ears were listening to Father's words on eternal life with God.

"Park there, Caitie," General Nana says, pointing to an open space a block before the funeral home.

"How about I drop you off at the door and come back here to park?"

"Park there, I said." She pulls down the passenger visor and checks her bright pink lips. She adjusts her hat. "Gawd, here we go. I'm supposing that I'll have to talk to that woman!"

"Who?" I get out of the car to go and open her door. "Who will you have to talk to?"

"Why herself, of course. The woman who cremated your father and wants my body, too. She knows I have to come here for my wake. It's the closest one for all my friends to get to."

I have had it. Had it to the limit. "Look, Nana, can't we let this rest? You're a healthy woman. You have a lot of years left. Why even think about this stuff? It's morbid. Truly."

"Morbid it is, huh? Look here, lassie, don't give me sass! You're here to learn. As for the Missus, I'll handle her. Maybe I'll arrange to be put out at the funeral home in Canaltown. That's not so far from here and Store Patch. And, I heard they do a better job on hair and make-up. Oh wouldn't that fix her! She'd be all ready to come zip me up in a bag and bring me here, providing you issued a check, mind ya. And, instead, you'd call Vincenzo's hearse to come get me. Oh, yes, I'm liking this idea."

I'm smoking. Furiously puffing. My toes are curled inside these insidious black pumps. "Fine. Whatever you decide will be fine." I don't tell her that her pre-occupation with her own death is cause for worry. I don't mention that I intend to talk with my sisters and my Uncle, her son, about her behavior today.

"Damn right it will, and you'll make sure my wishes are carried out. You were real good about making sure your daddy's did."

Inside, we each sign our name in the register. When she turns to hand me the pen, Nana says, "Make sure, every one, I mean EVERY one, signs my books. I don't care how many ya gotta use up. I suspect you'll need at least two. And everyone who signs gets a thank-you card from you. Get your sisters and your aunt and cousins to help write them out. I want them written out, not stamped or put through one of your high-tech pomcuter things.

"Computer, Nana."

"Yes, well, just make sure you get a lot of cards, and make sure you don't wait long in getting them out."

Gritting my teeth to keep my mouth from opening, I smile. I follow her in to the room wherein Maggie is displayed in her casket. Nana strolls up the isle between two rows of folding chairs, almost all of which are occupied by those who had been in Maggie's living room. As usual, I feel my knees turn to jelly. I hate kneeling in front of dead people.

"And a suit? Why the hell would I want to be in a suit, the most uncomfortable clothes man ever designed? What a friggin' waste of

time and money. Dressing the dead! I don't want anyone staring at me and saying how good I look. Good? How the hell can you look good? You're dead, for Pete's sake!" I hear daddy's voice as though he were next to me, here, at the kneeler in front of poor old dead Maggie in her cream-colored, lace-trimmed dress. I want to laugh, so I lower my face to the top of the kneeler.

"Nana taps me on the shoulder, a sign that it is time to move on. She has said her prayer, I guess. I feel goose bumps form when Nana touches Maggie's hand and says "good-bye." I touched my grandfather like that just a couple of months ago in here. His hand was cold and hard, like rock. Not at all like the big, strong, warm hand I remember holding on our way to church Sunday mornings.

I stand, feeling guilty because I did not pray for Maggie's soul while I was kneeling. I even forgot to bless myself before I got up. More marks on my long list of sins. At best, I am a cafeteria Catholic. I pick and choose what I want to believe of Catholic doctrine.

Nana opts for us to sit in the middle of the third row, in clear view of Maggie. "You see the spray above the casket, Caitie? That's where I want your Uncle Bob's floral tribute to me to go. Above me. Red roses.

"What if Uncle Bob doesn't want red roses?" I feel like slapping myself for having asked. Now, she has me!

"He will. He damn well better. I left money and instructions."

There is a buzz of human noise. Not every one has taken a seat. Many are walking around, hugging and kissing and laughing with old friends and family they evidently have not seen in a while.

"Yiz know, boyo, it stinks that we only see the lot of you when somebody dies. Yiz only live 15 miles away. It ain't like yiz can't drop by for a visit," Neal Boyle says to his cousin, Sean Devlin.

"Aye, and it ain't like yiz can't drive those 15 miles north to my place," Sean says. "Besides, we got more to do up there in the little city. That's why yiz should come to my place."

Nana is listening to the exchanges. "Ain't this grand, Cait? Why more than even I expected turned out for Maggie. Look at them. They're having a great time. I sure do hope I get this kind of turn out. I hope I die around check day. Every one comes out then to get their Social Security and do their shopping. Why if that happens, you might need three or four guest books."

This is a family reunion. A celebration of life. I have yet to see any one shed a tear. "Nana, why isn't any one crying?"

"Ah, hell, Caitie, Maggie was old. Lived a long, long life. It'd be different if this were a funeral for a young person, ya know. Don't sound so glum. Pay attention to what's going on. Besides, they'll cry tomorrow when the casket closes and at the graveside. That's when death really sinks in.

"Which reminds me, you make damn sure, lassie, that my pallbearers are grandsons-in-law and people who I like. I don't want no drunkard off the street paid to take me to the grave."

"Promise, Nana. Even if it means I have to carry you myself." I say this with sincerity. I think. I couldn't possibly have meant for it to be as brash as it sounded to my ears. Could I?

"No need for cockiness. Besides, you can't. You're a woman. Men have to carry the body."

"Says who?"

"What does it matter? That's the way it has always been, and as far as I am concerned that's the way it will be at mine."

The busy buzz becomes a hazy hum when Father O'Malley arrives with Bible and Rosary in hands. He kneels before the body, talks with Margaret and other immediate family and then takes his place at a lectern, which is more ornate than the one from which he pontificates in our church.

Mrs. Politawicz stands next to Father. "Every one, please. We are going to get started with . . ."

I can't hear what she is saying because Nana is making gutteral sounds.

"There she is. That bitch."

"Shh. She'll hear you for crying out loud, Nana!"

"Makes me want to live to be a hundred or at least longer than she's going to live."

I have to turn my head. I am holding back a laugh. It wants to come out so bad that I am crying. Mrs. Yanewich, seated behind me, hands me a tissue.

Father is working on beginning the Rosary. I can't bear the thought of sitting here much longer, if for no other reason than sitting bores me stiff. "Nana, look, I need to stretch. I am going to go have a smoke. You'll be okay, here?"

"Course, I will. Go mingle in the smoking room. Not every one will be in here, praying, though praying would do you some good, Caitie."

I'm going to pray I make it through this night without losing my sanity. I am going to smoke until my lungs fill up and my head goes empty. I am overwrought with concern for Nana. Had I known what this day was going to be like, I would have made an excuse not to come. Not for this. I know she has to die some day. I am prepared for that. But I'll be damned if I can deal with what she's brought upon me today. I'm a photographer. Not a mortician.

I smile at attendees whom I know, but I don't stop to gab. Outside, I walk to the corner and sit on the middle step leading up to one of the doors that is not in use tonight. I realize Maggie is in her coffin on the other side of that door when I hear Father O'Malley leading his flock through the Sorrowful Mysteries. I can smell candle wax and carnations on the night air.

Trying not to think about Nana, I allow my mind to take a walk back in time. My time. I grew up in this old coal town. Now, I hardly know a passer-by. In fact, the funeral home and Holy Family Church are the only places I visit when I come to Ferndale. I read in the *Fairlane Journal* that the Bishop is closing the town's Catholic school, where I went as a little girl. Enrollment is down even further. That's the story in all of our little towns around here. It's a damn good thing His Excellency the Bishop does not operate our fire companies. Not that our volunteers would stand for so much as consolidating their resources . . . *Amazing how a mind can wander from one thing to the next just to avoid the matter at hand. Nana.*

Bodies pour out of the funeral home. I assume this is a sign that the wake is over. It is time to collect Nana and take her home. It's adrenaline keeping her on the move today. Usually, she's a bed by nightfall, if not before.

We are invited back to Maggie's house. On behalf of Nana, and my sanity, I decline the offer. Nana does not insist otherwise.

She yawns as I drive south on Route 209 toward Store Patch.

"In my closet, there's a plain pink dress. I ordered it from QVC. That's what I want you to give to the undertaker to bury me in. I bought it just for that, and after seeing Maggie in that cream thing, I know I made the right decision."

I do not acknowledge receipt of this information.

"You hear me, Caitie?"

"Yes," I say. "I heard everything you said today, but I don't understand why you are engaging in such depressing activities. I think you need to get out more. Go back to senior citizens or something."

"That's simple."

"I don't think the seniors are simple. I thought you liked the gatherings. Just because Ida Kraus pissed you off . . ."

"I'll thank you not to use such vulgar terms, lassie. Very unladylike. And that's not what I meant."

"Well out with it then. What did you mean?"

"The answer to why I am making sure that my send off is perfect is simple."

"Oh? And it is?"

"I want to make sure everyone knows I was loved. I don't want to be forgotten."

Afterword

"Coal is like character, the deeper you go into it, the more interesting it becomes," said geologist David White.

So it is with coalcrackers, people born in northeastern Pennsylvania's historic anthracite region. Coalcrackers are "the stuff" of which life is made and books are written. They work hard. They play hard. They do not quit. They like to tell stories, and there are plenty of stories to tell.

Coalcrackers are a proud, strong and friendly people whose folks — immigrants who came to America in search of a better life — made American industrial and social history. Their ingenuity, creativity, labor and stubborn will built a place that thrived, struggled, crashed and is now being reborn. Today, they are a people rebuilding their communities to reflect their resilient spirit and their belief that most things are possible through hard work and faith.

Coalcrackers are located far and wide. They serve in the military. They hold executive positions in Fortune 500 companies. They are inventors, doctors, lawyers, musicians, skilled tradespeople, statesmen, working mothers and housewives. As far as their dreams may take them from here, most coalcrackers never forget their beginnings as people of modest means and tremendous potential.

Years ago, when the area lost its economic backbone, many coalcrackers left in droves and vowed never to expose their origins. Today, these same people are no longer ashamed to say they were born and raised in the Pennsylvania Anthracite Region.

With today's modern communication, many coalcrackers receive e-mail from individuals who have roots in coal country and just "want to talk with somebody from home" or from "God's Country."

Not only are coalcrackers blessed with a history rich in culture, they also live in one of the most beautiful regions in the nation. Mountains, forests, streams and rivers are plentiful. Even the culm (coal waste) banks are beautiful in a unique way. Ask any coalcracker who played "King of the

Mountain" or climbed to the top to slide down these manmade hills.

Despite that their lives may seem worlds apart from mainstream metro areas, coalcrackers are bound to people outside "the region." Sure, there are places here that seem virtually uninfluenced (some would even say "untainted") by modern ways. Despite their nuances -- such as the vernacular -- coalcrackers laugh and cry, win and lose, triumph and make mistakes, like all people, everywhere.

In my work, I seek to incorporate regional cultural history in stories about contemporary coal region life. Various narrators tell the stories in Book One. These characters are representative of people whom one would meet in coal region communities.

Book Two features Cait Beck, a woman born and raised a coalcracker. Compelled to help her aging grandmother, Cait relives some of the best traditions and qualities born in the coal region. Family is important here. Old-style family dinners, Sunday church-going and family activities are a mainstay of life in coal country.

If my fiction piques your interest in anthracite region culture and history, there are many fine reference books available. I encourage you to access these. Please utilize the list of recommended material as well as Internet links that follow.

Meanwhile, I hope you enjoyed the coal region and the characters you met in these pages. I welcome your comments and encourage you to contact me at cgoldie@epix.net or via snail mail at 39 E. Centre St., Shenandoah, Pa., 17976.

Please also visit:
www.homestead.com/INKable/index.html.

About the Author

Christine M. Goldbeck is a former photojournalist, columnist and newspaper editor who has won numerous state awards and one national award for her writing. She is also a published, award-winning poet. Her work has been published in "Pennsylvania Magazine," "The Irish Edition," "The Writer," and "Now & Then" as well as in "Tales of the Mine Country," a book by Eric McKeever. She lives and writes in Shenandoah, Pennsylvania.

David Naydock's art appears on the cover as well as on the opening pages of Book I and Book II.

About the Artist

Born in Pottsville, Pennsylvania, May 29, 1960 and raised in Pittsburgh, David Naydock is a self-taught artist living and working in Pottsville. Working mainly as a mural artist, David has done more than 60 such projects over the last 15 years (23 in Pottsville alone) and was featured in the May 1996 issue of "Pennsylvania Magazine." David also has done many easel paintings, portraits, landscapes, collages, graphics and abstract paintings, more than 600 of which are in public and private collections throughout the United States, Canada and Australia.

The author expresses special thanks to Edward E. Shank, sculptor, of Middletown, Pennsylvania, who drew the scene on Page 17 for "Proud to be American".

Recommended Reading

Note: The ensuing list is comprised of reference volumes as well as historical fiction novels. By no means is this a complete list of the many books available about the Pennsylvania Anthracite Region. Many of the books in my list also contain excellent bibliographical information. With the following information, I aim to provide the reader a broad point from which to begin his or her reading. Enjoy!

Tales of the Mine Country by Eric McKeever
The Knox Mine Disaster by Robert Wolensky, Kenneth Wolensky and Nicole Wolensky
Growing Up in Coal Country by Susan Campbell Bartoletti
When Coal was King by Louis Poliniak
The Kingdom of Coal Work, Enterprise, and Ethnic Communities in the Mine Fields by Donald E. Miller and Richard E. Sharpless
Once a Man Twice a Boy No. 9 Mine: Driving, Closing and its Rebirth as a Tourist Mine by David Kuchta
A Molly Maguire Story by Patrick Campbell
Nine Bells at the Breaker ... an immigrant's story by Geraldine Glodek
The Coal Cracker by John Devers
Irish Day by Leo G. Martin

Coal and Iron (a labor story) by Leo G. Martin
Iron Steps by Donald R. Serfass
When the Mines Closed by Thomas Dublin
Panther Valley Tales by James Haldeman
A Guide to the Molly Maguires by Mark Major and H.T. Crown
Reincarnation of the Switch Back Gravity Railroad byWalter H. Niehoff II
The Valley Gazette (monthly newspaper strong on coal region history) Gazette Publications, 102 W. Water St., Lansford, Pa., 18232

Anthracite History and Culture

Internet Links

Each of following sites provide many links to anthracite history and society information.

www.minecountry.com

http://www.tnonline.com/coalcracker/

http://www.f-tech.net/irishmusic/

http://www.history.ohio-state.edu/projects/Lessons_US/Gilded_Age/

http://www.coalregion.com/

Preview

Mollie's Diaries
by Christine Goldbeck

An exploration . . .
Of five generations of women in the Pennsylvania anthracite region

An adventure . . .
in the politics of family and community

A story . . .
of hope, love, loss and renewal

CHAPTER ONE
March 20, 2016

Some one I once loved told me diaries are self-serving, subjective ravings of crazy people. Perhaps, some are. Mine never served that purpose. Were it not for tablets and pencils, I would be insane. Blank pages are good listeners and even better mirrors of the spirit within. Spirits are many-sided and, if allowed, ever growing.

Dear God, please let her be mature enough not to hate me when she reads those outpourings of my heart and soul. I am going to suggest she do that. Am I seeking absolution? Can the chronological account of misery and hope, trial and error, love and loss, betrayal and retribution help her? I hope so. God, please let it be so.

For all the creations I have birthed, Emily, my blonde, brown-eyed beauty, was the best thing I made in life. I raised her as well as I knew how. It was not like I had good examples to follow. I know I made mistakes. What mother doesn't? Even normal mothers do.

Of course, Mollie you are hardly one to define normal. You're lucky you can spell it, really. Normal is what? A big house, surrounded by a perfectly rigid fence. See, there you go. Normal people like fences around their homes.

Normal be damned. You've had one hell of a life so far, and you know it. So it's not been normal. It has certainly been eventful, even adventurous. You might as well add dangerous and scandalous to the list, at least for those years between 18 and 31. Go ahead laugh. And, be glad you can. It beats the days when you choked back tears and struggled to maintain even a smidgen of sanity. Tears were the price for nonconformity, for dedicating your life to breaking an age-old pattern and creating a new formula.

It's been a trial run. Some times, the experiments blew up, shattering my heart and my hopes but never my spirit. Oh, the spirit bled here and there, but it never died. Pain, poverty, embarrassment, nor anything worse - and there was "worse" - could kill it, not even forsaken love.

If I had the chance to go back, would I do things differently? Funny, no matter how many times I have asked myself this question, I always decide that I would not. Not for the money. Not even for the security. Knowing what I know now, I might do it for love. Might. I must be getting soft in my old age. Twenty years ago, not even love would have done it. I had been there and done that . . .

"Mollie, telephone. For you. T'is Emily."

"Thank you, Mrs. Flannery. I will take it here."

"Happy birthday, Mom. Pick you up at the airport Sunday?"

"Thank you, sweetheart. I am having the time of my life."

"You're not coming home. Are you?"